Rosamond Lehmann

INVITATION
TO THE
WALTZ

*With a new Introduction
by Janet Watts*

Published by VIRAGO PRESS Limited 1981
20–23 Mandela Street, Camden Town, London NW1 0HQ

Reprinted 1982 (twice), 1985, 1988, 1993

First published by Chatto & Windus Ltd. 1932

A CIP catalogue record for this book
is available from the British Library

Printed in Great Britain by
Cox & Wyman Ltd., Reading, Berks

ROSAMOND LEHMANN

(1901–1990) was born in Buckinghamshire, the second of the four children of R. C. Lehmann. One sister was Beatrix Lehmann, the actress; her brother was the writer John Lehmann. She was educated privately and was a scholar at Girton College, Cambridge. She wrote her first novel, *Dusty Answer*, in her early twenties. In 1928 she married the Honourable Wogan Philipps, the artist, with whom she had one son and one daughter. In 1930 her second novel, *A Note in Music* appeared. *Invitation to the Waltz* followed in 1932 and its sequel *The Weather in the Streets* in 1936. Both were dramatised as a BBC TV film in 1983. During the war she contributed short stories to *New Writing*, which was edited by her brother: these were published as *The Gipsy's Baby* in 1946. *The Ballad and the Source* was published in 1944, followed in 1953 by *The Echoing Grove*, which was to be her last novel for many years. Rosamond Lehmann then wrote an auto-biography, *The Swan in the Evening: Fragments of an Inner Life* (1967), and in 1976 she published another novel, *A Sea-Grape Tree*.

Rosamond Lehmann was one of the most distinguished British novelists of this century. She was a Vice-President of International PEN and of the College of Psychic Studies and a fellow of the Royal Society of Literature. She was made a Commander of the British Empire in 1982.

Virago also publishes *A Note in Music*, *The Weather in the Streets*, *The Gipsy's Baby*, *The Ballad and the Source*, *A Sea-Grape Tree* and *The Swan in the Evening*.

VIRAGO
MODERN
CLASSIC
NUMBER
53

INTRODUCTION

When Rosamond Lehmann published *Invitation to the Waltz* in 1932, she was already a star. Her first novel, *Dusty Answer*, written not long after she graduated from Girton, had been a *succès fou* when it was published in 1927: acclaimed by reviewers for its exceptional literary qualities, and devoured by readers for its exposure of a young woman's varied and powerful passions. Those critics who chose to take a line of lofty moral disapproval only helped further to boost the book's popularity and sales.

Miss Lehmann recalls: 'The shock was tremendous. I couldn't believe it. It sort of bowled over the public and the critics, and people were suddenly saying, "Here's a new kind of writer, and she's saying new things." Alfred Noyes wrote that it was the kind of novel that Keats might have written, if he'd been alive at the time; and Rose Macaulay – who afterwards became a great friend – wrote a somewhat censorious review saying that when she was at Cambridge, she and her friends never thought about young men.'

Rosamond Lehmann didn't enjoy the publicity which, paradoxically, made her less sure of herself and of what she was trying to say. Instead of increasing her self-confidence, it sapped it.

It crashed in upon an early life sheltered in the bosom

of a cultivated Edwardian family, in the peace and beauty of a riverside house and garden at Bourne End in Buckinghamshire. Rosamond Lehmann's mother was a girl from New England, with all that country's characteristic attributes of stoicism, moral strength, uprightness, and devotion to duty; her father, who was considerably older, was a distinguished man of letters, a Liberal MP and an eminent athlete, descended from a long line of painters, musicians and writers. He was Rosamond Lehmann's earliest mentor and her strongest first influence, the constant encourager of her creative efforts from childhood onwards. At the same time both her parents were of the opinion that 'Girls should be pretty, modest, cultivated, home-loving, spirited but also docile; they should chastely await the coming of the right man, and then return his love and marry him and live as faithful, happy wives and mothers, ever after' as she wrote in *The Swan in the Evening*.

Their daughter was at least partly disposed to agree with them. Yet by her twenties Rosamond Lehmann had already found herself an unwilling harbinger of revolution and change: unhappily married, childless, separated, about to be divorced. Now this publication seemed to expose her as 'a frank outspeaker upon unpleasant subjects, a stripper of the veils of reticence; a subject for pained head-shaking', as far as the older generation of her relatives, friends and neighbours were concerned; while in the contemporary world of letters – 'a world I had burst into unawares' – she became 'the recipient of lyrical praise, of rapturous congratulation, of intense envy, of violent condemnation'.

Both as a woman and as a writer, Rosamond Lehmann

continued to surprise people throughout her life. In later years the shocks were to take a very different form. Her psychic and mystical experiences and investigations into the paranormal following the sudden shattering death of her daughter disturbed the very intellectuals (Bloomsbury-based) who had been her early champions. But well before that, while she was still a young writer, her sequel to *Invitation to the Waltz* – *The Weather in the Streets*, published four years later – followed its delightful young heroine (now a lot older and apparently not much wiser) into an illicit love affair, an unwanted pregnancy and a backstreet abortion. This was strong and not altogether welcome stuff for the British public of 1936, and was even less welcome in America.

The controversy over these early books upset Rosamond Lehmann a little; 'but more than anything, it surprised me.' While writing them she had never considered the effect her novels might have on their public: it had not occurred to her that people might be shocked by them. She now finds it hard to believe that anybody ever was.

In a short story she has described the way her novels have evolved. Having been all her life 'a privileged person with considerable leisure,' she writes,

'leisure employs me as a kind of screen upon which are projected the images of persons – known well, a little, not at all, seen once, or long ago, or every day; or as a kind of preserving jar in which float fragments of people and landscapes, snatches of sound.' Each one of these shapes and sounds 'bears within it an explosive seed of life . . . Suddenly . . . one day, a spark catches, and the principle of rebirth contained in this cold residue of experience begins to operate. Each cell will break out, branch into fresh organisms . . .' The novel grows into life. Its life is its own.

In all her novels, Rosamond Lehmann says now, 'I just wrote what seemed like the truth in my experience. It was something inside me – an enormous complex of experiences and emotions, my own and other people's, that I had to give expression to.'

As she acknowledges, the experiences and emotions were (at least at this stage of her writing life) those of women rather than men. It was women in their predicaments – poignant, joyous, humiliating, and comic – that she put at the centre of her work. In her novels we discover, or remember, or realise afresh, or find ourselves finally laughing at what it is like to be an adolescent girl, a woman undergraduate, a mistress, a mother, a daughter, a sister, a wife. It is no accident that the majority of Rosamond Lehmann's readers have always been women; and their letters have told her that the most important thing they have found in her books has been themselves. 'Oh, Miss Lehmann, this is my story! – how did you know?'

In the body of her work, *Invitation to the Waltz* is a *divertissement*, almost a side-step out of Rosamond Lehmann's essential world, the theatre of private human passions. Nobody even quite falls in love within its pages, rare indeed among her novels, and there is much comedy in the action.

Olivia and Kate Curtis, the daughters of a prosperous rural middle-class household in the England of 1920, grumble, gossip and daydream a week away until the coming-out dance of an aristocratic local neighbour. They live through the eventful hours of the dance itself, to emerge into their separate and subtly-changed to-morrows. No more than that. We are privy to painful torments in the heart of the engaging Olivia, but as far as everyone else and the action of the story are concerned, they have no importance or even existence. They remain masked by the modest front of a well-brought-up young *bourgeoise*.

Invitation to the Waltz is a miniature framed, enclosed and perfected by its anachronism. In almost all the details of its outward appearance it is a period piece. The English upper middle class no longer occupies houses substantial enough to provide schoolrooms where daughters may be educated privately by governesses (as Rosamond Lehmann and her sisters were) or lounge at their ease for an afternoon of sewing and speculation. Villages no longer boast the sort of seamstress who will be thrilled to cut out a first evening dress for one of these young ladies, or ragged children who will sing after her impudent snatches of doggerel. Debutantes may still be given dances in the country houses of England, but the girls who attend them will be younger in years and older in experience than our endearing heroines, and it is unlikely that their revels will end in a thermos of cocoa before retirement to Bedfordshire.

Yet there is something extraordinarily familiar about Olivia Curtis's painful enjoyment to readers who have never attended a first dance in a great country house. Anyone who has nerved himself or herself to make a bottle-bearing debut in a threadbare student flat or set of festively-paperchained municipal offices has known what Olivia has to go through. Beneath the froth and frolic and false smiles of *Invitation to the Waltz*, Rosamond Lehmann presents to us the agony and the comedy of every neophyte's initiation.

> From the sanctuary of the bedroom, from thick rugs, whispering voices, soft lights and mirrors, four-posters strewn with wraps of velvet, fur, brocade, they emerged – crying in their hearts Wait! Wait! – wishing to draw back, to hide; wishing to plunge on quickly now, quickly, and be lost, be mingled . . .

Who hasn't once been Olivia Curtis, trapped in her bright dress that so disastrously fails to fit her body and soul? Exposed to the casual mercies of a capricious fate for what seems like the happiness or doom of her life, in an unending succession of good, bad, or unbearable moments; thinking, planning, keeping moving; delighting, despairing, daring to hope . . .

Outwardly, nothing much happens in this novel; inside Olivia's head and heart, the action is intense and fast-moving. Nobody can see it, but the reader can hear it in the audible small talk counterpointed by the rapid inward jabberings of Olivia's unquiet mind. Olivia's conversation with the congenital malcontent Peter Jenkin, consists mainly of what she thinks and feels and tries not to feel, without speaking a word of it.

In her stilted interchange with another disappointing partner we hear, echoing louder than a hunting-cry, Olivia's shame at her tumble into the trap beyond a class barrier –

> 'I'd rather have a good day's hunting than a week's shooting, any day.'
> 'Yes, I quite agree. It looks so lovely, too, doesn't it? The red coats.'
> 'The what?'

INTRODUCTION

'The colour, I mean.'

He said very distinctly, looking straight in front of him:

'Oh, the pink coats.'

'Yes, the pink coats.'

She tried to repeat it indifferently, as if correcting what of course had been a mere unaccountable slip of the tongue ...

The whole story moves through dialogue. Kate Curtis gracefully steers her own ineluctable course. In the exchange of monosyllables in the book's final conversation, we may listen to something enormous happening: a family's power structure shifting, a character changing, a world ending and beginning:

Kate said with peculiar calm:

'The Heriots want me to dine and go to the hunt ball.'

Abruptly her mother's face altered. In a flash all was as clear as day. She said quickly at random:

'When is it?'

'Tomorrow.'

'Just you?'

'Yes.'

'We must talk it over.'

She got up to go, voice, manner, her most authoritative, most non-committal.

'I said I could,' said Kate.

In *Invitation to the Waltz*, as in all her novels, Rosamond Lehmann's world is the human heart; and this book, like all the others, moves through the rapid and delicate course of human emotions. This is a book about daydreams and raptures and frantic inward miseries dissolved in the fraction of a second by the modulation of a voice, the glimmer of a smile, the quiet cool air of an evening garden. In this novel perhaps more than any of her others, Rosamond Lehmann is writing about the delights of being alive, the pleasures that, even when one is seventeen and badly dressed, irresistibly redeem its pains.

> She saw the glinting stream running between the garden and the park. The spaces of sky and lawn were broad and peaceful. Trees, water, moonlight made up their own cold world, unalterable, infinitely detached from humanity. It was like dying for a bit to be out here . . .

With the same vitality and the same completeness, Rosamond Lehmann transmits the loneliness and humiliation on the dark side of an evening's radiance. It is her great gift to involve her reader in emotions that are painful and grotesque, yet through words that seem to flow from a deep sense of well-being in the writer, which the reader also finds himself sharing. At once we share the pain that is expressed, and the pleasure of its expression. It is a remarkable experience. She is simply one of the most enjoyable English writers to read. We suffer with Olivia at the nadir of her despair: yet we would not have it a word or a minute shorter than it is –

> Surely he had seen her. His eye, vague and rapid, had rested on her for a moment and passed on. He seemed not to recognise her. She moved to a better position for being noticed. First she sat down, then she got up and stood against the wall. She watched him, in a panic, without seeming to watch him. Her heart-beats grew so loud and rapid, she felt she must choke. After the second encore she went out of the ballroom into the passage, walking right past him. He glanced at her quite blankly. He must have mistaken the number – he must. And it was impossible to go up to him because of all those others. It can't be true. It's too much to

bear. How can I live if things like this are going to happen?

The agony that is also agony for the reader, and yet is not agony at all, is swiftly gone. We draw breath with Olivia again – the breath of the evening air, the breath of relief; we feel with her the death of hope and the death of disappointment. Then that moment too is gone. The empty terrace of escape has become a new scene with a fresh character. The next thing is beginning to happen.

Rosamond Lehmann's memory is hazy about a book she wrote almost half a century ago: but she does recall that when she came to the meeting between Olivia Curtis and Rollo Spencer, the glorious elder brother of that house, upon its moonlit terrace, 'I thought, I see! *this* is what all this is about! I think I realised there was an awful lot more to say about Olivia's life – an awful lot that I didn't yet know, and must wait to find out; and that meeting was unrealised, it was broken off. But I knew that *that* was what I'd got to deal with later.'

In a few years' time, the reader will meet Olivia Curtis again: fined down as fashionably as she could wish, and humorous and valiant as ever in the face of defeat that is perhaps not defeat at all. But that is another story, which we too must wait to find out. Until then, *Invitation to the Waltz* – as its author justly considers – is 'a very complete little work: and a very cheerful one'.

Janet Watts, London 1981

CONTENTS

Part I,   *page* 1

Part II, *page* 115

Part III, *page* 151

PART I

PART I

THE village, in the hollow below the house, is picturesque, unhygienic : it has more atmosphere than form, than outline : huddled shapes of soft red brick sag towards gardens massed with sunflowers, Canterbury bells, sweet-williams.

There is a pump on the green ; also a tall historic-looking lump of granite whose origin is wrapped in legend. Some refer it to the Druids. Some say King Charles I. sat down upon it.

The village of Little Compton is old, but the square stone house is new. It was built at the same period as Tulverton paper-mills, towards the middle of the nineteenth century, and was primarily designed to shelter the old age and accommodate the numerous offspring of Mr. James Curtis, first founder of the first mill. Tulverton is three miles away. Mr. Charles Curtis, eldest son, rode there and back upon a grey mare, day in, day out, during the pro-

longed period of his prime ; at the last, clad
in lavender-grey frock-coat and top-hat, every
inch Mayor of Tulverton, he brimmed daily to
and from the office within the dignified compass of a brougham. Moving with the times,
his son Charles James covered the distance
upon a bicycle. Perhaps his only son James
Charles will drive there in a motor car. But
times are changing. It is the year 1920 ; and
James, last fruit of a late marriage, is but seven
years old. Victim of overwork during the war,
his father has retired at sixty in poor health ;
a gap yawns for the first time in the line of
direct succession. Distant relatives and relatives by marriage and such as are not relatives
at all assume authority. Besides, nowadays
who knows what boys will grow up to be, to
want or not to want ? What happens to the
descendants of those Victorian grandees ?
Where are the young men ? The mould is the
same, but it is cracked : the flavour is strange ;
it dissipates itself ; is spent. Perhaps the last
James will never have a car and go to and
from Tulverton mills.

The square house is screened from the street
by a high clipped hedge of laurel. Passing the

drive gate you see, at an obtuse angle, and through the branches of a flourishing Wellingtonia, glimpses of slate roof, spacious windows, glass porch with coloured panes. And at once the imagination is engaged. You see rooms crowded with ponderous cupboards, sideboards, tables ; photographs in silver frames, profusely strewn ; wallpapers decorated with flowers, wreaths, birds, knots and bows of ribbon ; dark olive, dark brown paint in the hall and passages ; marble mantelpieces vapid, chill, swelling as blanc-mange ; the water-colour performances of aunts and great-aunts thick upon the walls ; worn leather armchairs pulled up to hot coal fires : you smell pot-pourri and lavender in china bowls ; you taste roast beef and apple-tart on Sundays ; hot scones for tea—dining-room tea on the enormous white cloth, beneath the uncompromising glare of the enormous central light. . . . But there is something more than this that strikes you, makes you linger. What is this current, this penetrating invocation flung out from behind discreet and tended shrubbery ? All is sober, is commonplace, conventional, is even a trifle smug. It is a pre-war residence of

3

attractive design, with lounge hall, etc., and usual offices, beautifully timbered grounds, well-stocked kitchen garden. Yet there is no mistaking the fascination, or its meaning. Something is going on. *The kettle's boiling, the cloth is spread, the windows are flung open. Come in, come in! Here dwells the familiar mystery. Come and find it! Each room is active, fecund, brimming over with it. The pulse beats. . . . Come and listen!* . . . Yes, we are sure of it. These walls enclose a world. Here is continuity spinning a web from room to room, from year to year. It is safe in this house. Here grows something energetic, concentrated, tough, serene ; with its own laws and habits ; something alarming, oppressive, not altogether to be trusted : nefarious perhaps. Here grows a curious plant with strong roots knotted all together : an unique specimen. In brief, a family lives here.

It is impossible to resist. There is the name upon the gate : THE LODGE. The orange gravel drive sweeps up in a steepish incline, and rounds a circular grass plot before the front door. And there in the middle of the shaven grass is the monkey-puzzle tree. And

there on each side of the door are the fuchsia
bushes, with the buds all popped by James, and
before him by his sisters. And there growing
up the side of the house, neatly framing the
dining-room window, is that kind of thick,
bristling, woody, point-leafed shrub with tight
clusters of orange berries. And there inside
the glass porch is the blue-and-pink tiled floor
and the couple of blue hydrangeas in tubs ;
and the umbrella-stand.

The inner door is closed. It is winter.
Quarter to nine in the morning.

§ 2

Kate burst open the door of Olivia's bedroom and looked sharply round, with anticipatory distaste, expecting to see what indeed
she saw. The customary richly rounded mould
of blanket presented itself to her ; the customary dark swirl upon the pillow marked the
approximate position of her sister's invisible
face. She paused ; but as usual this mould,
this blot, remained inactive.

She said loudly :

' Quarter to nine ! '

5

Reluctant upheaval, slow collapse and elongation of the shape. Then in a languid way she said :

' Well . . . many happies.'

At once Olivia replied alertly :

' Thanks.'

Her voice cracked. She lay silent, plunging and groping through thick waves of torpor, and coming suddenly upon her birthday lying at the bottom, a shut, inviting shell, waiting to be picked up and opened. She unclosed one eye and looked at Kate.

' A small token of esteem will await you at breakfast.'

' Oh, *thank* you ! '

Duty done, Kate reverted with a snap to harsh briskness.

' That is, if you're able to sit up and take notice by then. Really, I believe you'd never wake up at all. Now, don't go off again. Remember what Mother said yesterday.'

' What ? '

' She'd have to start calling you herself.'

Olivia gave a hoarse chuckle.

' Thought for the day . . .'

' Well, she will, too.'

6

' Surely I'm allowed an extra half-hour on my birthday.'

Kate reflected, and in justice conceded this.

' Well, buck up.'

She vanished with a deliberate slam of arousal.

Another five minutes, thought Olivia, and shut her eyes. Not to fall asleep again ; but to go back as it were and do the thing gradually —detach oneself softly, float up serenely from the clinging delectable fringes. Oh, heavenly sleep ! Why must one cast it from one, all unprepared, unwilling ? Caught out again by Kate in the very act ! You're not trying, you could wake up if you wanted to : that was their attitude. And regularly one began the day convicted of inferiority, of a sluggish voluptuous nature, seriously lacking in will-power. After I'm married I shall stay in bed as long as I want to. Girls often marry at my age. Seventeen to-day.

Thinking of the birthday, she felt all at once wide awake. Was it possible that one could ever stop feeling a bit excited as December came round again : could ever say as Mother had said when James presented the potted

7

azalea : 'Oh dear, I thought I'd given up having birthdays?' . . . and James had wept.

Oh, but breakfast would be awful, with all the family saying many happy returns ; with opening parcels, repeating thank-you with self-conscious strained enthusiasm. . . . This was the sort of occasion which, in old days, had caused Mademoiselle to raise eyes and hands to heaven, exclaiming : '*Ah, quel pays ! Quels sans-cœurs !* ' Dates would be celebrated with thoroughness ; handkerchiefs, gloves, flowers bestowed ; the Christmas tree decorated, the Easter egg *entamé* : but the spirit was all wrong, she said ; and as the day of festival wore to a close, she wept for her parents, aunts and uncles, brothers and sisters, nieces and nephews; and alternately clasped and rebuffed her embarrassed pupils ; and finally wrapped her head up in a purple woollen scarf : so that all one's life that harsh, crying colour would be the colour of homesickness ; that perforated, viscerous crochet pattern the portrait of a *migraine*.

Only one more week now till the Spencers' dance.

She got out of bed with an exhilarated swoop, and started to dress.

Her windows looked west over part of the lawn to the walnut tree with the swing in it, and some beds of massed shrubbery, and behind them the belt of elms dividing the garden from rough fields ; and beyond all these, low grass hills and ploughed lands flowing away with their telegraph poles and haystacks into the distance. There had been gales ; and now every branch was bare at last, December-naked ; but to-day a carved quietness in the tree-tops, a luminous quality glowing secretly behind the white veil of air, promised the weather she liked best : windless, mild, faintly suffused with sun. The landscape looked serene and wan, as if it had begun to draw slowly out of exhaustion into the crystalline purity and delicacy of convalescence, replenishing itself in peace after the agony of trees, the driven cloud-wrecks, the howl, the roar of the whirling dark—all the huge idiot pangs of ceaseless effort and resistance. Looking back upon those storms, she felt them as one long uneasy listening of her whole being for the return of stillness : a tension like incessant undirected prayer : *let the noise stop, oh, let the trees have rest.* She had feared, seeing from the windows the walnut tree, that old tower of benevolence, casting off its domesticated, protective character—its role of swing-bearer, mild avuncular tolerator of grip and scrape of the raw climber, ample host to the secretive adolescent armchaired in bole, laid along bough with book, block, and pencil, bag of caramels—to wrestle austerely, with catastrophic incongruity, in elemental struggle. She had suffered for the shallow-rooted elms, listening in the night for their doom. But now, there were all the trees, intact, far from disaster, stark islands of tranquillity. Out of the heart of them rose and fell the rooks over and over again, like slow dark thoughts of peace.

Happiness ran over like the jet from a sudden unexpectedly spurting little wave. Birthday and fine weather in conjunction : the omens were propitious.

Which of the two jumpers—the crimson, the fawn ? The fawn to-day. The crimson heartened the lesser days, put a firm face upon them. It suited her, as they said. But to-day she could suit her clothes, provide the glow, fill out the shape, warm up texture and colouring. She pulled on her brown stockinette skirt, regretting, but without irritation to-day, the slight bagginess at knees and bottom ; fastened a broad scarlet patent-leather belt. The belt was an object that had virtue in it. She had had it for two years. It was cracked, peeling a little. Within its compass she felt a certainty of individuality, like a seal set on her, and she loved it, liked to think of it lying coiled, secret and brilliant, in the top left-hand drawer. She had another belt, a thin nigger-brown one of suède ; and that was a good belt too, though less dependable.

She cast a glance at her figure in the long glass ; but the image failed her, remained unequivocally familiar and utilitarian.

Nowadays a peculiar emotion accompanied the moment of looking in the mirror : fitfully, rarely a stranger might emerge : a new self.

It had happened two or three times already, beginning with a day last summer, the languid close of a burning afternoon ; coming from the burdened garden into the silent, darkened house : melancholy, solitary, restless, keyed

up expectantly—for what? waiting—for whom?
The house was empty. She took off her creased
linen frock, poured out cold water, plunged
her face and arms. She must put on a new
frock—her new raspberry-ice-pink cotton frock
with short sleeves and round neck, just back
from the dressmaker. The rough crêpe stuff
clung, she smelt the faint pungency of fresh
unwashed cotton. She looked in the glass and
saw herself. . . . Well, what was it? She
knew what she looked like, had for some years
thought the reflection interesting, because it
was her own ; though disappointing, unreli-
able, subject twenty times a day to blottings-
out and blurrings, as if a lamp were guttering
or extinguished : in any case irremediably
imperfect. But this was something else. This
was a mysterious face ; both dark and glowing ; hair tumbling down, pushed back and
upwards, as if in currents of fierce energy.
Was it the frock that did it ? Her body seemed
to assemble itself harmoniously within it, to
become centralized, to expand, both static and
fluid ; alive. It was the portrait of a young
girl in pink. All the room's reflected objects
seemed to frame, to present her, whispering :

Here are You. She felt the quiver of the warm sun-drained air like the swim and beat of pulses in soft nervous agitation. Roses and leaves breathed in the window ; and the evening bird voices seemed to circle with exultant serenity down the sky, like the close, the completion of some grand inevitable freeing design which she both created and took part in.

She went on staring ; but soon the impression collapsed ; the urgent expectation diminished flatly. After all, the veil was not rent. It had been a false crisis. Nothing exciting was going to happen. There was nowhere to go : nobody : nothing to do. In the glass was a rather plain girl with brown hair and eyes, and a figure well grown but neither particularly graceful nor compact. . . . But hope had sprung up, half-suppressed, dubious, irrational, as if a dream had left a sense of prophecy. . . . Am I not to be ugly after all ?

Now I'm seventeen I shall begin to fine down. . . . But supposing one never did fine down ? There was Kate, who had never had phases. Long lines had acquired light curves with effortless simplicity, and a grace which home-made jumpers might blur but could not conceal. It was unfair that she should have such an easy life; though of course when accused she said she had plenty to worry her : the shortness of her eyelashes, a spot on the chin now and then, a red V at the base of the neck in summer. But what were these details compared with a blemished whole ?

She brushed her long hair, fastened it back with a large imitation shell slide before taking a last look at the general effect. Still a bit out of drawing, still swollen with sleep. And Kate woke up pink, clear, fresh, every feature the right size, so that one could not help thinking, most reluctantly and secretly, of flowers . . . of that thing, one of Father's two recitations :

> Mais elle était du monde où les plus belles choses
> Ont le pire destin ;
> Et rose, elle a vécu ce que vivent les roses,
> L'espace d'un matin.

Fair, classic, rosy, cold, the daughter of du Perrier had risen up in a moment from the grave, from the page of the exercise book, irrevocably fitted with Kate's face.

Recite that to me once a week, he had said

in the earliest French days; and he had
actually come creaking upstairs to the schoolroom, volume in hand, to see about it; had
benignly recited, caused Mademoiselle to flutter
and sparkle, to congratulate him on his accent,
to hope suddenly, visibly, for the best after all
in this English venture. What a queer man!
In those days one never knew when he would
show off to advantage; when the reverse.
For instance, when the Martins came to tea he
called them his apple dumplings, and that was
delightful for everybody: for the fat Martins
to have notice taken of them, for his daughters
to have such a joking father. But then he had
come to fetch them once from a party dressed
in a black mackintosh cape and the most
shaming German hat with a little feather in it.
He played the flute. As a boy, he had spent
summer holidays walking through France and
Germany playing for his bread and butter,
sleeping on haystacks, under hedges. He
walked through legendary villages at evening,
playing on his flute, and all the people came
running and tumbling out of their houses and
danced after him. That couldn't be true
really: the clothes, the setting belonged to

the Pied Piper. All the same she saw him clearly, indestructibly : his shock of hair, his shabby eccentric coat, his face of a queer bird, melancholy, heavy-lidded : (a lean bird then, a plump one now). How did it all fit with having to go to the mill with Grandfather and learning to be a business man ? . . . He hadn't enough breath now for the flute, poor Dad ; but he went on reading French, German, English—odd books, memoirs, essays, maxims and things, not novels. He said *On meurt beaucoup . . . et ce n'est pas encore fini.* He started off all at once, in measured, lofty murmur :

> It is not death that some time in a sigh
> This eloquent breath shall take its speechless
> flight,

—on and on, his voice emerging at the close to breathe out solemnly in mournful warning :

> And when grass waves
> Over the past away, there may be then
> No resurrection in the minds of men.

And afterwards he seemed to listen to the echo in the silence.

Oh, Dad—Kate ! . . . It wouldn't do. They

were garlanded, crowned with flowers, with death. At nine o'clock in the morning they were beginning to be mortal, to be precious. It wouldn't do. She stopped thinking about them, thought about the Spencers' dance instead ; left the room and ran downstairs two steps at a time. Outside the dining-room door she paused to brace herself, to prepare for the birthday. Then she went in.

' Here's our birthday girl.' Kate threw the helpful mock-salutation over this morning's Pip, Squeak, and Wilfred.

Smiling nervously, Olivia glanced at her plate. It was set with parcels : everything was in order.

' Mor*ning*.' She bent over her mother's chair to kiss her.

' Good morning, dear.' Mrs. Curtis's voice had a strong birthday flavour.

' Morning, Dad.'

She kissed him behind the city page of the *Times*.

' Morning, Simpk.' She lifted up the Pekincse from his advantageous central position upon the hearthrug, and squeezed out of him a prolonged snore.

But James, who had been hovering, standing on one leg and then the other, watching, listening in frantic dumb anxiety, now burst out :

' Many happy returns of the day !' For nobody, nobody had said it, and it must be said, or how could presents be opened ?

' Thank you, James.'

There was still Uncle Oswald.

' Morn*ing*, Uncle Oswald.'

And the usual problem presented itself : whether to kiss him, shake hands, pat his shoulder, or ignore him : for he was the most embarrassing person in the world, with his long soft stares, his secret nods and becks, his knowing winks and enigmatic throat-clearings. Finally she held out a hand.

Out shot his hand to meet her with peculiar covert swiftness and pressed her palm for a moment ; then as swiftly withdrew, leaving between her fingers—horrors !—a ten-shilling note.

' Oh, Uncle Oswald ! . . .'

Blushes suffused her. These he relished to the full, looking at her with the oddest expression, as if he guessed with delight the cause of her distress. For her hand had gone out so eagerly, as if—oh dear !—as if in expectation. Why didn't I pat him on the shoulder this morning ?

' There's a lucky girl.' Kate stepped again into the breach. ' Pop it in your money-box.'

James clutched her hand.

' Let's look ! How much have you got ? Paper ! Crumbling jumbos ! *Paper !* ' He screeched, fell on the floor, flung his legs up. ' I reminded him—didn't I, Uncle Oswald ? It was me who reminded him. I told him something else too. D'you remember, Uncle Oswald ? About what I saw—you know—the——' With violent contortions he mouthed: ' *Birthday cake.*'

' Hush, James, hush, that'll do. Get up. How very generous of you, Oswald. Olivia didn't at all expect it. Did you, dear ? '

' Of course I didn't expect it, Mother ! '

Olivia's voice went sharp. The birthday trembled while Mrs. Curtis thus summoned before them all the unquiet spectre of Uncle Oswald's poverty. For it was the chief thing about him. Nobody ever forgot it for long.

And so he had thrust a hand out with peculiar, with covert swiftness. . . .

Kate said with restrained menace :

' Olivia has now reached her eighteenth year, Mother.'

But :

' Look out of the window, James dear,' said Mrs. Curtis, passing on serenely, absorbed now in nature. ' Two dear tomtits in the new cocoanut. Isn't that nice ? '

James did not look out of the window. His perforating gaze was bent upon the parcel which Olivia was undoing. He took a sharp breath.

' That's from me.'

' Oh, James ! . . .'

It was . . . What was it ? . . . A piece of china, an ornament, a creation—a small bowl upon the edge of which sat an orange-haired cherub clasping to his nakedness two life-size purple pansies and some loops of dark-blue ribbon.

' Look, everybody ! ' She held it up. It was hard not to catch Kate's eye. ' Did you ever see anything so wonderful ? '

' Charming,' said Mrs. Curtis.

' Chose d'art. Chose d'art.' Mr. Curtis looked gravely over his glasses.

'Undoubtedly,' said Uncle Oswald. 'Hmm!' His voice, heard so rarely that it came always as a surprise, was a sort of breathy squeak. He looked quite brisk for a moment.

Slowly James examined each face, his bright blue gaze contracting with suspicion.

Suddenly Kate snatched it from Olivia and said :

' Boo, I'm jealous. Can I have it, James ? '

Then it was all right. Watching his sisters wrestle, he shone immediately with placid radiance.

' No, you can't, Kate. It's not your birthday.' He added gently : ' I'm afraid . . .' for it was a painful thing to have to say. He took it and handed it back to Olivia. ' Here, you can put it on the schoolroom mantelpiece, then you can both see it.'

He sighed and turned away. It had been a long job, but it was over. The expedition to Holloway's had been solemn, notable, the choosing dramatic, the paying anxious, the concealing tense. Each night a serpent voice had whispered : 'Keep it yourself. . . .' But now the final placing by the plate had been accomplished : all was over.

Olivia fumbled with the big parcel, feeling beneath her fingers a shape, a yielding body which might mean—must mean—what had been half promised : some stuff to make a frock for the Spencers' dance. Next moment out yawned a roll of flame-coloured silk.

'Oh, *Mother !*'

Tears pricked her eyes.

'From Dad and me, dear.'

'Oh, *Dad !*'

'What's that ? '

'Such a glorious present ! '

'Present ? What present ? Who's having presents ? '

'Olivia,' cried James, in burning reproach. 'It's her birthday.'

'Why wasn't I told ? How can I give presents if nobody tells me to ? '

'I can't be telling you everything,' said James bitterly. 'Why don't you keep a birthday book ? '

'Hush, James. Daddy doesn't mean it.'

'Dad's cracked another joke, James, that's all.'

' The *colour* . . . my favourite colour.'

Mrs. Curtis said deprecatingly :

' I should have chosen a pretty pale pink or blue. I like a young girl in delicate shades. Sweet-pea colourings : Aunt May and I always wore them. This seems a bit strong for a first evening-dress. But Kate insisted.'

' Yes, I chose it,' said Kate languidly. Her taste was law. ' What's the good of putting Olivia into girlish shades ? She'd only look sallow and ghastly. There's no reason why she should wear feeble colours simply because I have to.'

The sisters standing shoulder to shoulder looking at the glowing material communicated without word or glance. *It's what you wanted, isn't it ? Oh, perfect. Thank you, thank you.*

' I do love it.'

' Well, you must take it to Miss Robinson and get her to make it up in some very simple way.'

Mrs. Curtis endeavoured by a special tone she had to damp down the sensational element in the gift ; to deprecate the trivial question of evening-dresses. Yet an indulgent smile lit the imperious aquiline benevolence of her features.

'Boo!' cried Kate. 'I hate you. You'll look nicer than me.'

'Oh, I *shan't*——'

Of course that was out of the question. All the same, to break in flame upon the Spencers' ballroom . . .

She opened the last parcel : a fat leather diary with a lock, from Kate.

'*Just* what I wanted. What a beauty!' It must have taken a lot of Kate's money : such broad thick paper ; room for every kind of private document ; absolute secrecy. 'What ripping presents I've had.'

She sat down with relief to her boiled egg. The birthday had closed down officially until tea-time.

The Pekinese rose from the hearthrug, paced with ritual deliberation towards Mr. Curtis's chair, sat down beside it, and gave a loud trumpeting snore. Mr. Curtis laid aside the *Times* to gaze fondly at him, looked at his empty plate, looked down again, shook his head slowly, sadly.

'James.'

' Yes, Dad.'

' The little fellow's famished.'

' He's not.'

' Indeed he is. Not a crumb has passed his lips since Monday.'

' Who told you so ? '

' He did.'

' Oh well, he's telling fibs again.'

' James, James. Come here. Look into those lustrous eyes. Then dare to speak such wicked words again.'

Dutifully emerging from his private world, James came and looked.

' He only asks one kidney on toast or a small sausage. No devilled dragon's legs or anything tasty of that sort.'

James sighed.

' Try him with some of this magic toast.' He offered a corner of crust left on his own plate.

The Pekinese stiffened, recoiled in overwhelming nausea, then accepted the fragment, held it for a moment bulging in his cheek, dropped it on the carpet, stalked away again.

' Now we have hurt his feelings, James.'

James said a trifle impatiently :

' He'd eat it if he was hungry.'

' Really,' said Kate, ' since Dad retired he's
got awfully feeble-minded. He thinks about
nothing but Simpkin. It's an obsession. If
you'd heard him yesterday telling Dr. Martin
the most long-winded boring story about Sim
meeting a black cow and thinking it was his
grandmother or something. . . . Dr. Martin
thought you were loopy, Dad.'

' I know that story,' murmured James, busy
again with his meccano. ' Sim dashed up to
the cow and the cow gave a blow through
his nose and blew Sim over. Daddy did
laugh.'

' Sim's stolen our birthright,' said Olivia.
' I'm sure Dad never told stories about us. In
fact he loathed us.'

' In fact he still does,' said Kate.

Mr. Curtis looked mildly round upon his
family, got up, put the *Times* under his arm,
coughed his asthmatic cough, called to his dog,
and creaked away.

Mrs. Curtis gathered up her letters and
moved smartly towards the door. The set of
her shoulders announced the doom of leisure,
shamed the replete lingerer.

' Now, what are we all doing this morning ?
I have to go into Tulverton by the 10.30 bus.
James, it's your nature walk, isn't it, dear ?
Tell Nannie to get you ready *before* Miss
Mivart arrives, not after.   Otherwise you
waste time.   What have you got to do,
girls ? '

' Nothing.'   Kate yawned, stretched.   ' Read
a book, perhaps.   Or else just sit.'

Mrs. Curtis was silent : a pregnant silence.
Kate was going through a phase.   Best not to
take too much notice.

Alarmed, admiring, Olivia wrapped up the
red silk and said :

' I shall take my stuff to Miss Robinson.'

' Come, James, Mother's waiting.'

' Oh, bother my beastly old nature walk.'

' Come, dear.'

' Last time I only got one silly old hip.
And Miss Mivart wouldn't let me turn somer-
saults on the railings.   I don't like my nature
walk.'

Mrs. Curtis placed a hand upon her son's
shoulder.   Pouting, rubbing his face, he was
passed from the room.

Kate broke the silence, murmuring :

'Dash it all, it is the hols. As a matter of fact, I'm going to stoke up the schoolroom fire and do some sewing.'

Uncle Oswald was still there, standing by the window, lighting his pipe. The girls looked at him, he looked at them, his glance slipping from one to the other with that odd complicated expression he had—half withdrawn, half intimate : mocking, caressing, sharply inquisitive. He shook his head, drawing at his pipe and smiling slowly, slowly ; and their answering smiles seemed to flood the room with a sudden warm light. But this was in fact the sun, breaking at last through the grey and falling on their faces.

He came and stood in front of Olivia, his stubby tobacco-stained finger tapped on the diary.

'Now where shall the little key be hidden? On Uncle Oswald's watch-chain for safe keeping?' There was a world of insinuation in his voice.

'I wouldn't trust you.'

She laughed gaily ; but picturing that key dangling upon his paunch, at the disposal of those plump secretive paws, those pages naked

28

at night beneath the opaque scrutiny of those caramel eyes, she felt her blood freeze.

' A young girl's innermost thoughts, her dreams. . . . What could be more delightful? '

' What could be more idiotic ? ' said Kate.

' Though sometimes—sometimes,' he whispered, eyeing Olivia innocently, cunningly, ' sometimes I wonder if I mightn't—perhaps— be—just a *trifle*—shocked ? '

She said hurriedly, feeling a blush begin :

' Oh, Uncle Oswald, you were an angel to give me that ten bob.' (That was the worst of him. Beneath everything he said lurked the kernel of a blush, and sooner or later it was bound to begin to sprout.) ' You really oughtn't to have bothered. It's far too much.'

At this his face contracted, became a thing of wood. He waved a hand, silently departed.

Kate sighed.

' Funny old fish. I really do like him best of our relations. He's not a *complete* bore. In fact he's rather sweet.'

' Yes, he is. But don't you sometimes feel he's *slightly* sinister ?—that prying, hinting way he will go on, as if he was trying to grab at one's thoughts ? '

' Oh, that's all put on. It's his sense of humour. I don't take any notice, so he concentrates on you. Poor old object, I wish he didn't look so unappetizing. He simply doesn't know the meaning of the word dirty-clothes basket.'

' I suppose that's why he could never get anybody to marry him.'

' I might go and keep house for him in London next winter, after I've finished Paris. It 'ud be a way of getting to London. I'm sure he'd love it. Mother'd have kittens though, I suppose.'

' I wonder what he does in London ? '

' I believe he's a sort of librarian or secretary to some one—now and then.'

' It must be very now and then. He's nearly always here. And I'm sure Mother doesn't like having him. It's queer. I asked Dad once if it was true he was awfully brainy : because I'd heard somebody say so : Aunt Edith, I think. And Dad said : He was once ; but after he left school he never had very good health. Dad sounded awfully sorry somehow. I didn't like to ask any more. But I suppose that explains him.'

And they meditated upon his one food-spotted old black suit, his finger-nails, the dead grey hair falling over his grubby striped flannel collars ; upon his mysterious London existence ; upon the hint in the air—never explicitly on any tongue—that life had long ago somehow counted him out, labelled him *Damaged* ; and that, for this obscure reason, there was forbearance but no welcome in their mother's reception of him ; and in their father's, something which he alone appeared to call forth : a kind of gentle solicitude ; the faintest, most delicate indication of a desire to protect.

After a while, Kate said carelessly :

' I heard from that Kershaw creature.'

' What ? . . . Oh ! . . . Why didn't you . . .' No use railing. It was just like her. ' Well ? '

She took from the pocket of her jersey a letter written in a minute and meticulous hand upon cream-coloured paper stamped with a blue college crest. Olivia felt a tremor as she read :

DEAR MISS CURTIS,—

Many thanks for your letter and invitation. I shall be very pleased to come and stay for the dance on the 17th. It is most kind of you to ask me. Please remember me to Mrs. Curtis. —Yours sincerely,   REGINALD KERSHAW.

' Hmm. He doesn't let himself go, does he ? You can't tell much from that. What a lovely handwriting ! '

' Do you think so ? A bit finicky, to my mind. Bank clerkish. Spotty, with glasses. " Most kind "—that's distinctly shady. It's what Miss Mivart would say. Why couldn't he say how ripping of you. . . . Oh, he'll call us Miss Curtis the whole time and amble round the room kicking our only slippers and pumping our arms up and down and clutching our skirts up in a lump at the back so that the backs of our knees show.'

' Shut up. I don't think he sounds a bit like that. Much more the athletic sort who can't express themselves. Big and fair, with lovely teeth and a deep energetic rather abrupt voice. Kershaw sounds awfully footballish.'

' Ah, but what about Reginald ? . . . Chin chin Reggie ! I feel I *must* call you Reggie My mother knew you when you were *just* a wee woolly bundle. . . . Ugh ! . . . Still, I suppose we must thank our stars.'

' Of course we must.'

For now the dance was safe, and anticipation could range free. Now they were at least ' and partner ' : though the plural requested by the invitation card had proved beyond their powers. In spite of Marigold Spencer's airy encouragements over the telephone : ' Come anyhow. We only put partners so as to have some over for the puddings,' it had seemed too deep an humiliation to have to confess to total failure. Yet daily, hope had dwindled. There were no partners—at least no possible ones, said Kate with angry tears : thinking of those three Heriot boys on top of the hill—those handsome and dashing, those eminently desirable partners, so near, so far, so obviously the very thing, so unprepared to be so—shooting down from London, from Oxford to discharge guns in adjacent fields, to ride in point-to-points, to dance at hunt balls, all with such utter disregard of the existence of neighbours, such whole-hearted absorption in the starry galaxy plucked for each occasion from other brighter skies. They would certainly be going to Marigold's coming-out dance ; as certainly be having a house-party for it.

But Mrs. Curtis, after rebuking Kate, had forthwith started to devote the energies of a powerful mind to the question of partners. For an invitation from Meldon Towers was not one to refuse : Sir John and Lady Spencer were on the board of, in the chair of, at the head of every committee in the county, an admirable couple, shedding a wholly beneficent public glow. Shortly afterwards she had remarked with a reminiscent smile : ' Your grandfather was very strict indeed. Aunt May and I never went anywhere without a chaperon. No young man was ever allowed inside the house.' And then she had added, actually added : ' To his knowledge . . .' and looked aside with some roguishness. Also she'd said with a sigh : ' We were very fond of dancing. Bournemouth was a gay place in those days. I dare say it still is.' And with these words she had risen up suddenly before her daughters, not as she was—not matronly, dignified, rather ponderous in action, not absolute domestic dictator, censor, not queller of giggling-fits, detector of subterfuges, swift snubber, just admonisher—but fond of a laugh, flirtatious ; whirling round flushed in the waltz and lancers;

but light, slight-waisted, with her hair piled up on top of her head : stooping in her low-cut puff-sleeved ball-dress to smooth and pat herself in the glass, thinking : ' Yes—pretty . . .' slipping out to post a letter on the sly, letting somebody in with laughter and whispers by the side door at Bournemouth. So that they thought with a new detached amusement and appreciation : no wonder she didn't trust her daughters. Time gaped behind them, severing her from them, illuminating the shape of a lively Miss West of Bournemouth, who, accidentally meeting a middle-aged Mr. Curtis at a complicated junction, had got carried away irrevocably with him along a new line to the place where she was now. Perhaps she looked back and thought with a sense of loss : how happy I was then ; comparing all she had now—husband, home, children —unfavourably with having nothing. And they experienced a faint uneasiness, rather as if the eiderdown had slipped off in the night, half waking them in dim discomfort. What on earth had caused their parents to marry ? What relationship lay buried beneath the appearance of temperate esteem, the habitual amicability with which they treated one another ?

The list of local young men was small, unfruitful, soon exhausted. It was then, when hope was paling, that Mrs. Curtis made the great decision : young men should be invited to stay. But in vain the net was cast abroad. Cousins, one naval, one military, and one on the stage (but only occasionally, very discreetly and obscurely so) all sent polite regrets Kate wept in the night. Olivia felt worried several times. Mrs. Curtis began to let fall philosophical reflections of a general and stoical character. Reggie Kershaw, son of an old school friend and one of a secondary or passive group of godchildren, lost sight of since the christening mug, had been remembered, recalled from inactivity, staked in a last desperate gamble. And they had won. Mysteriously, out of the void, they had fished up an authentic young man.

Kate sighed again.

' And all we know is he was such a bonny baby.'

' I bet she'll tell him so too.'

' I'm afraid it's no good hoping Mother's

36

old school friends could produce anything exciting. Why are they all widows who've had
such sad lives ? '

' Or cheery little women who've always
struggled so bravely . . . ? '

' It's too morbid. Olivia, shall we *ever* know
any men ? any one who's any use, I mean.
Mum's standards are so shatteringly low.
Always creatures we must be kind to because
they're albinos or because they've got hare lips
or impediments in their speech . . .'

' Or else because their poor mothers can't
afford evening-clothes for them.'

' In fact, Ask him because he hasn't got a
tail-coat is roughly her motto about dances.
Gosh ! It 'ud be just our luck if Reg turns up
in a hired dinner-jacket.'

But their cynicism was assumed. Already
they were busy wondering whether he preferred blondes or brunettes, which of them he
would dance with most, who would show him
his bedroom, whether it would be all right to
be seen coming to or from the bath in their
dressing-gowns, what they could talk about at
meals to be bright, to cover their father's
remarks and Uncle Oswald's silences. And

they were going through their limited ward-
robes—the fawn? the red? the green? the
grey and blue?—and thinking in what a
friendly sensible unaffected way they would
treat him : so that they would appear well
used to entertaining young men. And Kate
fingered her letter, and thought how curiously
attractive it was, the whole thing—the small
glossy cream page, the little blue crest, the
effect of decoration produced by the tiny care-
fully-spaced handwriting. It was thrilling. She
decided to keep it in her desk, for a bit anyway.

'Well, I suppose we must begin the day.
Violet'll be flouncing in to clear in a minute.'

'I'm off to Miss Robinson. Oh, Kate, I do
bless you. Supposing it had been a pretty
pale blue? Stoke the fire up against my
return. At this time of year young girls can't
be too careful.'

She looked out at the garden, at the frail
winter radiance falling on grey grass and
mauve crumpled earth of rose-beds, dissolving
branch and tree-trunk into shafts of muffled
light and shadow.

Yes, the sun's coming out. And it's my
birthday.

§ 3

The door was opened by old Mrs. Robinson : toothless, scored with wrinkles, exhaling the curious smell of an old woman. Something almost forgotten returned sharply : a lean figure, bobbing, misshapen, black woollen crossover pulled tight over bowed shoulders, white corkscrew ringlets and scalp showing through, tenuous voice hovering, pouncing out of the jaw's shaken hollow cave : *Come in, my dear ; come in !*—and the same smell at the door of a dark cottage : the frightening visits to the gardener's antique mother once a week with a pound of tea and sugar.

' I'll tell my daughter.' Old Mrs. Robinson's voice was grudging, pessimistic. ' She's been laying down with the nooralgia. I don't hardly think she's fit to see you. She's been bad all the week. I tell her it's her teeth, but she says she'd rather have the pain than let the dentist look at her. I don't know how it'll end, I'm sure. Are *you* all keeping pretty well ? '

' Frightfully well, thank you.'

' Ah . . . I'm glad to hear that. This weather's that treacherous, you never know.'

She opened further stops, increasing the volume
of her dirge. ' And I've been so poorly lately
with my old trouble. I don't know what it is
to get a good night's sleep. In fact, we've all
been poorly. If you'll just take a chair I'll
call her. But I don't hardly think she's
fit . . .'

I hate her, thought Olivia, left alone. It
was the same catalogue of complaints every
time. The Robinsons vied with each other in
chronic suffering. The air in the house was
heavy, lugubrious with their minor afflictions.
But old Mrs. Robinson and the eldest daughter
(the one whose weakness was in the head, who
never appeared and never did anything) and
the second daughter (the Post Office one) had
a store of meek and voluptuous Christian
patience on which to nourish disease ; and the
youngest, the dressmaking Miss Robinson, had
none. She had only her imagination.

Waiting in the chilly buff front sitting-room,
Olivia thought about religion. It was undoubtedly a fact that faith was failing. Nowadays, at the moment of getting into bed, when
a lifetime's habit still suggested prayer, one's
immediate reaction was a confused mental

protest, like an impatient shrug of scepticism ;
and straightway, a shade uneasy, into bed one
got and thought about something else. Gone
this many a day were those ecstasies, that
crouching low upon the pillow, eyeballs pressed
to palms, till stars and coloured globules
appeared, and one began to be almost sure one
was in the presence of God. Suspicious now
seemed that brief mystical period when a
shining white Shape had appeared one evening
among the flowers on the altar during Easter
Mission week : when one had fallen on one's
knees and thanked God for the Revelation :
and remembered to offer thanks again each
night at the same hour for a fortnight. There
was no savour left now in putting on best coats
and hats for church. The only point of interest
remaining was the spectacle of the High antics
of the new curate, his duckings, wavings, up-
risings at the altar—carried out with a kind of
ardent breeziness, a frenzy of disregard for the
outraged, flaming - cheeked, mouth - pursing,
head-shaking Lowness of his congregation.

But Kate had not lost her faith. She went
on getting up in the dark for Early Service,
breathing every response, sitting with a modest

pure attentive expression under her Sunday
hat brim beneath the streams of eloquence and
beams of fervour playing upon her from the
pulpit : for the new curate, whose eyes were
large and fanatically pale, had formed the
habit of fixing them upon Kate and preaching
to her alone. And though this was of course
a joke, it was sometimes a joke that didn't
quite come off : as if Kate were not quite so
amused as oneself ; as if she might be reserving
a secret satisfaction. Also she looked pure the
day the curate came to tea, and stonily refused
to respond when one caught her eye and
winked ; and said afterwards nothing disgusted
her more than vulgarity. God was taboo between them now : in fact, the whole family
avoided the subject. Dad was an atheist : so
definitely so that the sight of a clergyman
irritated him ; and one could say at school :
My father is an atheist ; while Mother delicately concealed her beliefs, if any, assuming
a curiously formal and reverent manner, un-
favourable to levity, at any symptom of the
subject ; and severely rebuking James when
he exclaimed Good God on seeing rice pudding
again. Nowadays it took James's nerve to

embark on religious discussion ; and the appalling nature of his spiritual problems, propounded always at meals, upset the entire family equilibrium. For Dad would lead him on and encourage him to pick holes in Mother's painstaking but evasive explanations, while Kate put on her we-are-not-amused face, and one giggled oneself, and James, incited by Dad, started to show off and had to be snubbed.

Some time or other I must think it all out, read some helpful books, really worry about it . . . Oh, but it can't be helped ! It'll all come right. Because, of course, I do believe . . . I believe—I believe in everything . . . sun, moon, stars, in seasons—trees, flowers—people, music, life . . . yes, in life. She was shaken with excitement, took a deep breath. . . .

Silence reigned in the house. Where was Miss Robinson ? Opening the piano with its fretwood and fluted pink silk face, she played a few muffled bars of *Little Grey Home in the West*, which topped the pile of songs upon the bracket. *Homing* was beneath it ; *A Broken Doll* ; *Two Eyes of Grey* ; *The End of a Perfect Day* ; *Indian Love Lyrics* ; dozens more—a rich collection. The youngest Miss Robinson, gay-hearted, quivering, hysterical, started away now and then from the odour of complacent dejection and sanctified decay ; but she could escape no further than to the front room and the twanging piano and the wild warbling of voluptuous ballads. This room, called now the fitting-room, she had won for herself : these four walls held the remnants of her freedom, her humour, her hope, like a wistful and dwindling presence within them. For she was sinking, fatally enmeshed, struggling feebly and more feebly as youth slipped from her year after year, and old Mrs. Robinson continued to be alive, and virginity, like a malignant growth, gnawed at her mind and body.

The floor creaked overhead : she was preparing to come down. Of course she would come. This was the hundredth time she had been prematurely extinguished beneath the murky parent wing only to emerge shortly afterwards at the top of her form. For, like the trumpet upon the war horse, the words Some one to see you acted upon her spirits ; and among her limited clientele Olivia was juiciest prey and first favourite.

Here she came now, her step lively, and

humming a little tune. Her eager beaming face shot round the door.

'Hullo, Miss Robinson.'

'Hull*aoh* ! I was expecting you. Saw you in the tea-leaves last night.'

'Did you really? I'm so sorry you've got neuralgia.'

She put her hand quickly to her cheek.

'Aoh, it's awful.' Her pale tranced bulging eyes stared mournfully. But immediately she added : 'Aoh, it's nothing much. It goes off and comes on. Couldn't be bothered to get up, that's all. Thought Gertie could do some work for a change.' She giggled, clapped hand to mouth, signifying a joke. 'Oo, it's parky in here. I'll pop and fetch the stove.'

She darted from the room, darted back again, negligently swinging a smoking Valor Perfection ; uttered a kind of bray on seeing the red silk which Olivia had spread upon a chair to dazzle her.

'Aaaoh ! Scrumptious ! What's that for? An evening gownd ? I never ! You'll look all right in that. Beautiful quality. No stinting this time either, from the look of it. Isn't it bright though ? The Scarlet Woman.' She winked. 'Whose choice was that, may I ask? Not Mother's surely?'

'No. It was Mother's present, but Kate chose it.'

'Aoh, Kate, was it? Well—it wouldn't be everybody's taste, but I like something out of the usual. Some can carry off something out of the usual, some can't. You can—though no one could call you a bewtee. Shouldn't mind seeing meself straoll into a ballroom in this. I always fancied flaime.'

She flung the material round her shoulders laughing to see, in the glass, her pale pared-away face of a hare incongruously top the dashing gypsy richness.

'Well, you'll be noticed in this, anyway. I don't say but what it won't give you more chance than those insipid shades. Your mother's not one for what I call show, is she?'

'Oh no.'

Olivia considered serviceable dark-brown or navy-blue winters, holland and tussore summers; cream viyella blouses, white piqué tennis skirts; all plain, neat, subdued, unbecoming. The patches of colour splashing one's wardrobe's life history were as rare, now

one came to think of it, as roses in December.
Each one remained vivid in memory : isolated
accidents, shocks of brightness : a crimson
ribbon slotted through an early white party
frock, exciting, evoking again the drop of
blood of the fairy story piercing the cold,
blank, startled snow, piercing her smooth mind
indelibly, as she read, with sudden stain ; an
orange Liberty scarf on a straw hat ; a curious
coat of violet frieze that winter of wearing
half-mourning for Mother's father.

Now that I'm grown up and can choose my
own clothes, I'll wear bright colours always.

' And oh, angel Miss Rob, can you do it for
next week ? It's for a dance.'

' A dance ! I say, you are getting on.
You'll be ever so gay before long, I suppose.
Aoh, aren't some people lucky ? Well, don't
forget—I'll make your wedding-dress.' Her
elastic features expressed excruciating amusement.

' I'll remember.' Olivia smiled, seduced by
the suggestion.

' Aoh, aren't some people lucky ? . . .'

Miss Robinson looked at her with hungry
curiosity: seeing perhaps lights, flowers, silks and

satins ; hearing music and the vibrating tones of gentlemen in evening-dress ; seeing rings, trousseaux, orange-blossom, and bridal lilies and processions : more or less the sort of glamorous effect produced in one's own imagination by the thought of Cousin Etty Somers moving against her mysterious London background.

When Etty came to spend a few days in the country with her cousins, and was arch and coaxing with Dad, and with Mother serious-minded, delicate, overtired, needing rest and Ovaltine, and lay smoking on the schoolroom sofa, and blew scent over herself from a spray, and gave them cast-off wisps of chiffon underclothing, too small for them, and staggered their straining ears with tales of kisses and would-be kisses—then romance was made flesh. Then they could but gaze, listen, hover, devoutly carry up the breakfast tray, could but lament the wretched contrast afforded by their own lives—the humdrum present, the dreary future. So perhaps Miss Robinson's fate appeared to her when she thought of the Misses Curtis. Poor thing. For the first time, Miss Robinson's life rose up objectively and faced her. Olivia saw it with dismay, with guilt. She made frocks for other girls to dance in. She would stay in this awful house, seeing the seasons change over this view of allotments, as long as she lived. Oh dear . . .

'Had you thought of any partic'lar style? I don't suppose you had. You aren't much of a one to know your own mind—not like Kate, are you? Here's the latest.' She wetted her finger and flicked over the pages of *Fashions for All.* 'What about this, now, with the draiping in the front? Or that's smart, look—the fullness both sides like a pannier sort of effect. That's distinctly out of the usual, isn't it?'

'Wouldn't it—mightn't it broaden me?'

'Well, it might. You are on the broad side, aren't you? Nothing to Mother, though, are you?—*yet.*' She winked. 'Well, I tell you. Have the draiping one side only and caught *here*'—she prodded Olivia's left hip—'in a graiceful bow. That 'ud take off from your hips.'

'And a flower. A big silver rose—or something.' Olivia woke up, clearly seeing a silver spray on flame-coloured silk.

'Aoh!' Miss Robinson shrieked, clapped

her hands. ' The very thing ! Well done you !
Slow but sure—I always say so.'

' I'll buy one in Tulverton.' With Uncle
Oswald's ten shillings.

' Aoh, we'll make you look posh. Those
tinsel blumes are so artistic. What about the
bodice, now ? V, rounded, boat, or square ?
And how much of your chest and arms do you
mean to expaose ? '

' Oh . . . not too much. . . .' She relapsed
into uncertainty, gazing in the glass at the pair
of knobs at the base of her neck, and the
protuberant ridge of her collar-bone. ' These
ghastly salt-cellars. . . . If only I could fill up
here and go down behind.'

' Aoh, cheer up ! How'd you like to be
blessed with a frontispiece like the Miss
Martins ? I can't hardly cut them a day V
without getting down to nature. Though if
it's a choice, I'd rather have that than Mrs.
Trotter's—aoh, don't speak of it !—right down
below her waist. I couldn't help remarking
to Connie last time I fitted her, her shape's
enough to put ideas into people's heads.'

She put a hand to her mouth, slid a glance.
An inner Miss Robinson seemed to peer out

suddenly, give a lewd nudge, whisper : Come
on now ! How much d'you know ? And for
a moment a whole train of surreptitious words
(such as fornication, and White Slave Traffic),
shameful images, obscure warnings (such as,
Never travel alone with a man in a railway
carriage) seemed—horrors !—about to become
pieced together into the Facts of Life and
slipped furtively into her hand by Miss Robinson. But next moment she had turned her
attention outward, the lid was safely on. It
was with her usual somewhat half-baked
brightness that she remarked :

' That young Mrs. Jones at the farm is that
way again, I see. Have you noticed her ?
And the last not a year. Aren't men selfish ?
I tell Connie there's worse things than being
single.'

Olivia summoned the arch disbelief expected
of her.

' All the same, you'll be getting married yourself one of these days, you know.'

' Aoh, go on ! Not I. Why, I'm a reg'lar old
maid now.'

She looked in the glass, smoothing her skirt
over her hips. She had a trim figure, rounded

and compact, and she wore her white shirt
blouse and navy-blue skirt with a little air
that gave them a distinct appeal. The colour
was starting to flame over her cheekbones.

Why shouldn't Miss Robinson get married ?
Though plain, she was prettier than some, she
loved a joke, could play the piano and sing,
was domesticated, warm-hearted, good-tem-
pered and generous, her nature craved affection. But she wouldn't get a husband : she
hadn't a chance now. She was thirty. Letting
I dare not wait upon I would, youth had gone
by ; and now the candour of her desires was
muddied, her spark of spirit spent. Never
would she do now what once she had almost
done : walked out of the house and left them
all whining and gone to London to earn her
living. That was after the death of Mr.
Robinson, an able cheerful man—manager of
a department in the mills, churchwarden, clerk
to the Parish Council. Though Connie said
We must all look after Mother now, and Gertie
under emotional stress lost what head she had
and needed special care, and Mother said I
need all my dear daughters round me now,
God willing we shall never part in this life, I

feel it won't be long before I too Go Home—
in spite of all this, she would—almost—have
gone, and been the selfish one, the undutiful, the
heartbreaker ; and never come back to Little
Compton again. But of course she hadn't
done it. She didn't even know now that she
disliked her mother. Enmeshed in those col-
lapsible leather tentacles, she felt comfortable,
developed poor health, had her nerves ; went
out only on Wednesday afternoons with Connie
for a little shopping and perhaps the pictures
in Tulverton : for they kept themselves to
themselves, finding, they said, all the society
they wanted in their own home. Then, too,
in a small place like Little Compton one had
one's position to consider : one had to be
wary, touchy, quick to take offence at fancied
slights or misplaced familiarity. One could
pass the time of day with the wife of one's
right-hand neighbour, a market gardener, but
not with the wife of the bricklayer on one's
left—a very common person. One could have
considered the offer of a Sunday walk with
the local bank clerk (who had never offered),
but never with the handsome young cowman
(who had) : so far forgetting himself once as to

accost Connie and Elsie in the lane and make that very suggestion. And though haughtily repudiated, who shall say how often it and the dark-eyed, broad-shouldered, full-lipped maker of it appeared, irrepressibly, in strange places and curious disguises, in the dreams of the Misses Robinson ?

Feverishly flicking over the pages of *Fashions for All*, she continued :

' I suppose I've had my chances like every-body else : more than some perhaps.'

' I'm sure you have.'

' I dare say I'm fussy.' She looked with *hauteur* at her own reflection. ' I always say, with a man you never know what you've got till it's too late, and then where are you ? Good husbands don't igzackly grow like black-berries, do they ? No. People don't know when they're lucky. I often think us single ones are spared a lot. Many a time Mother's passed the remark how thankful we should be to be together.'

The colour, darkening and throbbing on her cheekbones, began to come out in patches down her neck.

' Give us a song before I go, Miss Robinson.'

'Aoh, go on ! You don't want to hear my caterwaudling.'

'Yes, I do. Come on.' Olivia patted the piano-stool.

'Aoh, you are a one for setting me off.' She placed herself with alacrity upon the stool. 'What'll you have? The usual?'

Without more ado, she plunged into the opening bars of *Pale Hands I Loved*. Her voice was a shrieking nasal soprano, subject to long passages of acute tremolo. After this, she passed on with scarcely a pause to *Less Than The Dust*. A deep oriental drumming filled the room, the piano shook, the aspidistra quivered in its pink china pot upon the bamboo stand, the beads on the overmantel shivered and winked, the photos clacked against the wall. Miss Robinson swooped up, swooped down, recklessly leaping ticklish intervals. It was a short but very intense song. At the close she was considerably exhausted. Beads of perspiration stood upon her large pale nose.

'Wonderful ! Gosh, I wish I could sing and accompany myself. Dad says there's no accomplishment to compare with it, for a woman.'

Miss Robinson sighed.

' I've been too poorly of late to practise. I wasn't doing myself justice.' She brooded upon the piano-stool. ' If I'd have had better health . . . and if Mother could have spared me, I might have taken it up. We took a holiday at Brighton one August—some time ago now, before Father died. I must have been about eighteen. There was a gentleman in our boarding-house, a professional. Aoh, he had a scrumptious voice, a tenor. He would have it I ought to go in for it. He said I might go far with training and a natural gift like mine. But Mother was dead against it.' For a moment a faint echo of resentment sharpened her voice. ' She said my constitution 'ud never stand up against a professional life. He took me to hear Clara Butt sing on the pier once. It was lovely.'

Olivia nodded eagerly. Custom could never stale the Brighton gentleman. For one thing, his variety was almost infinite, especially with regard to age, colour of hair and eyes ; for another, Miss Robinson's feelings towards him were excessively unstable. Sometimes one teased her and she bridled, shrieked ; sometimes she inclined to cynicism. Now the affair would expand emotionally, threaten to become the Grave of Love, decked with sighs of discreet resignation and hints of everlasting fidelity ; now it would contract, stiffen disconcertingly into a Friendship : Platonic : not a subject for ribaldry. But through all the capricious metamorphoses of the Brighton gentleman one factor remained constant : his gentlemanliness. He had never gone too far, never made a tendentious speech, or snatched a kiss ; never in any way forgotten himself. He had taken her to the concert and brought her back again ; and so dropped stillborn, as it were, upon the doorstep in the act of raising his bowler in farewell ; and so vanished ; and afterwards been mystically reconceived and brought to birth by Miss Robinson. From out the dark phantasmagoric grove of her subconscious he would emerge, thither retreat for ever, assembling into many a shape and beckoning shadow ; but never again to be one and indivisible.

To-day, however, after a few moments' absentmindedness she brushed him aside of her own accord, banged down the piano lid, skipped to the window.

'Who's that passing? Mrs. Uniack. Ugly shape, isn't she?—so squat. They say she has very queer turns—change of life, you know. Her husband drinks something shocking. Some days he can't go to business—she lets on it's his war wound.' Miss Robinson uttered a hearty laugh. 'The airs she gives herself! Her father was nothing but a millhand—did you know? Of course he worked up—made his money. There's some funny tales about that too. He died of softening. I'm sorry for any one who has to nurse softening. Dreadful—so disgusting.' She grimaced. 'Looks nice out to-day. I might take a walk round. Haven't poked me nose out for a week.' She giggled. 'Too much trouble. Here's your hat. That new? Velore—not a bad shape. But you never did look your best in a hat. You haven't the knack. Now that Miss Cooper, she may be too sallow, but she can put a hat on. She looks reelly chick in that Sunday felt of hers. Well—you come on Monday for your fitting.'

'Right-o. Did we—did we settle about it?'

'Aoh, I'll draipe it on you, that's the best.

58

Don't you worry. We'll make you look posh.
You'll be cutting your sister out.'

'Oh *no*, I couldn't.'

'Aoh, cheer up. One man's meat's another
man's poison. You mayn't have the looks, but
you've got that sympathetic look in your eye.'
She winked. 'So she's off to Paris soon. Gay
Paree! Won't she have a time! And you'll
be left behind. Never you mind. You make
the most of it. I dare say it's very nice to have
a sister, but there's times when you can spare
one for a bit. . . .' She clapped a hand to
her mouth. 'Aoh, aren't I awful? But you
know what I mean. Take my advice and don't
miss your opportunities. Bye-bye. See you
Monday. Mind the step.'

Standing at the door, she nodded rapidly,
waved, her wan face creased with smiles.

In a moment she would go back, humming,
to fold the material, drink in the tonic of
its caressing brightness : for colours revived
her spirits, textures soothed her. She would
take it to show Mother and Gertie ; their
three heads would stoop over it. After a
bit she wouldn't feel so cheerful. She would
droop, get another shocking twinge in her

face, feel too poorly to go out to-day, shed
tears. . . .

Olivia shut the stiff little iron gate. She looked
back at the slate roof, gable, tile and stucco
façade, one of a row of three, the inscription
CARRICKFERGUS in white glass lettering above
the front door. The house on the right was
called WINONA, the one on the left DUNDONALD.
They were known in the family as Grandpapa's
houses : for Grandpapa, that beneficent poten-
tate, had built them, as well as the Parish
Hall in the same style. They stood aloof from
the old, the picturesque, the insanitary village
proper—examples of modern improvement ;
and much local prestige attached to them.
One must be very proud of all Grandpapa's
works. . . . She looked at them. But surely
—surely they didn't look very. nice ? . . .
in fact—horrid ? All that pretentiousness
and mincingness and mixture of materials.
Fancy Grandpapa having built such ugly
houses. She summoned the portrait in the
dining-room — the noble beard, the prosperous frock-coat, well-rounded waistcoat, all
the marks of his infallibility. She felt embarrassed for him, uncomfortable in her

family sense, almost guilty. Fancy criticizing Grandpapa.

At the upper window appeared the top half of old Mrs. Robinson. Mauve, sagging, spying, false, her face looked down from its habitual watch-tower.

She'll never die. If I come back in ten years, I'll see her sitting there, like a spider, just the same. And she'll come huddling down, wailing that her daughter is too poorly, too poorly. . . . Suddenly Olivia had a vision: Miss Robinson in a darkened room, the shutters drawn, the key turned ; and old Mrs. Robinson on guard, outside the door.

By God's will, in another ten years, Miss Robinson would be very poorly, very poorly indeed.

§ 4

She took the field path that ran up to the green, then down again past the farm to the foot of the garden. From the top of the incline she looked down and saw the village sitting in the faint sun. Smoke went straight up from cottage chimneys, and the women were hang-

ing out their washing. Patches of pink and
blue glowed among white patches. One line
had a yellow striped apron and one a scarlet
petticoat. There was something about the
look of the washing and the fences and the
arrangement of roofs behind—some thatched,
some tiled with old-gold, lichen-covered tiles,
all steaming and silvered with pale light—
something that made her wish to record it,
keep it somehow. It was the beginning of the
mood that led to wanting to write poetry.
Veils of illusion seemed to float over the
familiar scene, half-hiding, half-revealing it
under an eternal aspect. It looked like the
picture of the village, not like itself.

There in the distance was Mrs. Wells-
Straker, widow of widows, flowing, streaming
towards the church in all her crêpe. Was it
some Saint's Day, thanksgiving, penance or
commemoration known only to herself and
the curate? Or perhaps a private communing
with the late Mr. Wells-Straker. . . . For his
memorial tablet was the pivot of her life ; and
beneath it she sat, or with loud creaks and
rustles knelt, herself a monument, a Stygian
effigy, for some part of every day. Mr.

Smedley must find her fervour and regularity a great encouragement. Why then did he wear that distant patient look, as of suffering concealed, when he saw her waiting for him in the churchyard after service?

Olivia broke into an imitative jog-trot, then checked herself. It was her best imitation, but she oughtn't to do it. Mrs. Wells-Straker was so very kind ; and if she met one would gently call Good morning, dear ; and when she had asked after Mother, Father, and little brother, would say with loving sympathy : ' And so you'll be losing your dear sister before long. You'll miss her sadly, sadly, I'm afraid. Never mind, dear. Mother could never do without both her dear girls. Your turn will come, dear, all in good time.' And her voice would caress, console, approve ; make one feel good for staying at home and bearing the absence of Kate.

Never mind, never mind, my turn will come ! How would it come ? When ? Where ? Though she was to dance at Marigold's coming-out dance, though she as well as Kate had left Tulverton day-school, she was to consider herself no less a student. Kate was to go to Paris; but she was going to specialize: try for a scholarship to Oxford, perhaps, and then take up teaching. For all young girls should be fitted for a career; though Kate's remained by tacit consent unspecified. There was none that attracted Kate in the least. She wished simply to go to Paris for a year; therefore, since French was bound to come in useful whatever happened, to Paris she was going. But for Olivia there would be, in another few weeks, the early train to Tulverton again; the camel face of Mr. Blenkinsop (university coach), his mingling of subacidity, sawdust wit and cowering defensive bachelor ceremony. There would be the intractable miasmic swamps of algebra and geometry, the leaden hour between twelve and one—cold feet, Plato, aching back, Virgil, empty stomach protesting; and then joy!—the orange curtains, purple-and-orange check cloths, Art pottery, Art waitresses (mob-capped), pallid eggs and coffee, Chelsea buns of Pomona's Parlour. And then the post-prandial revival. In another few weeks she would retaste the flavour of Tulverton afternoons: French and German literature with beloved Monsieur

64

Berton, and twice a week the piano lesson—
delightful forty minutes' interlude : for she and
Miss Baynes, blonde, vaporous, most unexact-
ing teacher, had long ago come to an unspoken
agreement—Olivia playing her pieces for ten
minutes, Miss Baynes, in a gentle trance, for
thirty. Meetings, too, of the Literary Society,
arranged by Lady Spencer, vigorous promoter
of the cultural life, with lecturers of all kinds
reading such interesting papers ; or should a
lecturer fail, Shakespeare filling the breach,
parts assigned, a list of expurgations drawn
up beforehand by Lady Spencer to avoid
awkwardness, and sent round to each mem-
ber ; so that one's Shakespeare was scored
with injunctions to skip, skip, skip. Sitting
next to lazy ribald Marigold, who wrote
limericks and drew skinny Gingers in her notebook, and embarked with affected innocence
on censored passages, one spent one's time
giggling and frivolously conspiring with her
against the other members—the pudding-faced
girls, lean spinsters, prosperous matrons of
Tulverton.

The afternoons would hold their mounting
happiness. She would walk back to the station

for the 4.45 quite strangled sometimes with happiness made up unaccountably of opalescent dusk in the streets, and lamplight, and soon the blossoming almond, the crocuses in the public gardens, and shapes of roof and chimney-pot cut on the sky, and the footsteps of quiet people going home, and the remembered voice of Monsieur Berton saying with tenderness: My favourite pupil, and a muddled feeling of the importance of intellectual things, a determination to excel in—in what?—in serious subjects, in literature, music : to write a paper on King Lear and read it to the Society ; and, most of all, the remembered face of Marigold, that sketch in a few light lines, so simple, so mysteriously complex in its eliminations.

But now that Marigold was out, perhaps she would come no more to cast a luminous haze over the lecture-room. . . . And Kate, too, would be gone. The young and elderly men who got into the railway carriage to stare at Kate would get in no more. The journey home, the late tea, the schoolroom evenings would all be solitary.

Darling Kate—but I don't mind losing her

at all—not at all. I don't want to go with her
to Paris. I want to do something absolutely
different, or perhaps nothing at all : just stay
where I am, in my home, and absorb each
hour, each day, and be alone ; and read and
think ; and walk about the garden in the
night ; and wait, wait. . . .

Oh dear ! There was Major Skinner cross-
ing the cricket pitch towards her, with two
retrievers and a spaniel. She hastened her
pace. But :

' Hullo, hullo, hullo ! ' he shouted from some
way off, waving his pipe. There was nothing
to do but stop, and hope her blush would
arrive and subside before he caught up with
her. ' Where are you off to, eh ? What about
that lesson ? When are we going to have
that ? Here am I, waiting every day, always
at your service. . . .'

' Oh, thank you, Major Skinner. . . .'

She despaired, was dumb. For some time
ago, meeting her near the links, Major Skinner
had very kindly offered to teach her to play
golf ; and ever since she had had to avoid
him or try to make excuses. Broad-minded in
many ways though Mother was, for some

reason she drew the line at golf with Major Skinner ; and had been quite disproportionately annoyed when Olivia came home and announced the glad news.

'Well, what about to-day, what about to-day? No day like to-day. Jolly weather. You come along to the links this afternoon and we'll have a round.'

'I'm awfully afraid I can't to-day.'

'Oh, you can't to-day. Well, to-morrow then.'

'And to-morrow's Girl Guides.'

'Oh, Girl Guides, is it? What a busy little lady you are, aren't you? Always got something on. That's the spirit. Well, I tell you what : you give me a ring when you're free— see? You give me a ring.'

He was always hopeful, patient under disappointment. He looked her over ruminatively, lustful but gentlemanly, out of small blue bloodshot eyes.

'How's yer sister?'

'She's very well, thank you.'

'Hmm. Give her my salaams. Give her my salaams. And tell her—hmm. And yer father, how's yer father? What's he think of this Irish business ? You ask him from me. Tell him I'll come along and have a chat with him one of these days.'

' Yes, rather, I'll tell him.'

He sent this message every time ; but she had given up delivering it. It was somewhat oddly received at home ; and anyway he never came. He didn't ever send messages to Mother.

She bent to pat a retriever.

' Fond of dogs ? Nice brutes. You ought to have a dog, you and Miss Christabel.' He always called Kate Christabel. Perhaps, they thought, she reminded him of some one of that name whom he had once loved ; or perhaps he thought it suited her. Or perhaps he just got muddled. He hadn't a very good memory. 'Tell you what: next time Leila here has puppies you shall have one. I'll let you know, and you can come along, both of you, and have first pick.'

' Oh, *thank* you. It *would* be lovely.'

How kind he was. Oh dear ! One must just pray Leila wouldn't have any more puppies : for it wouldn't be allowed, it would certainly not be allowed ; and it would be so terribly awkward.

69

'Why don't you and yer sister look in on
my wife? Any afternoon. She'd be glad to
see you, y'know. It's a bit lonely for her down
here—after what she's been used to—in India,
y'know—though of course she has her pals
down from town . . . bridge. . . . D'you play
bridge?'

'I'm afraid not.'

'Ah, you ought to play bridge. It's a fine
game. A game of skill, y'know. Got to use
yer brains. There's an article you're not short
of, I'll be bound. Eh? You drop in for a
cup of tea one afternoon and get her to give
you a lesson.'

'I'd love to.'

Shame, despair again. Even though Dad
lifted his hat with particular courtesy when he
met Mrs. Skinner in the road, even though he
referred to her in a light, winking sort of way
as that glorious creature, Mrs. Skinner was
absolutely taboo. For she had a past: twice
married, twice divorced; literally dozens of
co-respondents; cause of at least one suicide
among Indian army subalterns; and now,
though long since withdrawn from the fray
into the obscure and indigent haven afforded

by Major Skinner and there dwelling blame-
lessly—even, it appeared, devotedly—somehow,
what with so much sherry-coloured hair, white
powder, vermilion lipstick, what with being
childless (after so many opportunities), smoking
in the village street, wearing such huge hats,
such high heels—somehow she had not con-
trived to become at all respectable. Or perhaps it was chiefly her voice, so ravishingly rich
and husky, tender as ripe fruit, mellowed by
years of gin and tobacco ; or her smile, so
surprisingly sweet, generous, inviting, breaking in her face like the undying flame of a
beauty almost swallowed up now in billowing
fat.

Anyway, it was being truthful to say one
would love to go. She and Kate were united
in their desire to make friends with Mrs.
Skinner. Not that they could altogether
condone the lipstick ; but one must be
tolerant. Probably she didn't realize in
her dark little Tudor cottage—re-christened
CHOTA-GHURR by Major Skinner—what a terrible lot she put on. Then the house was so
thrilling—quite unlike any one else's—full of
luscious green, blue, and purple cushions richly

trimmed with gold braid, and brilliant shawls
and pieces of embroidery, and huge signed
photographs, and heavy perfumes, and cigarette smoke : very exotic, as Kate said. She
was unconventional, that was all—awfully nice;
they longed to go to tea with her. But it was
no good : and Mrs. Skinner knew it. That
was clear from her manner when they met in
the street. Each time she seemed to shrug her
shoulders ; though all she did was to greet one
in passing with a friendly but ironic smile, a
tiny shake of the head at once humorous and
dignified ; and straight on she went, leaving
in her wake more than a whiff of camelia :
something impalpable that seemed to surround
her always, to trail after her, making hunger :
a promise of comfort ; as if, heaping the fire,
drawing curtains, lighting soft lamps, she were
saying in that voice of hers : Yes. Yes. How
foolish. What a pity. Never mind. Drink.
Eat. Rest. I know. I know . . . and so
smoothing out furrows of thought, brushing
away anxious questions.

Suddenly Olivia felt inclined to smile warmly,
lingeringly at Major Skinner. She did so. She
didn't care. He was a dear. She was attracted

by his human, his male quality—simple, sensual, kindly, pathetic. She was sorry for him, because all his offering was nothing but asking —tentative, shamefaced, pretty sure it was no go, but never altogether daunted. Poor old fumbling suppliant : he was getting old, he didn't have much fun. The nice, the fresh young girls avoided him, made excuses. By this smile she would make up to him for having to slight him.

The smile made really more of an impression than she had bargained for. He dropped his jaw, cleared his throat, blew his nose, pulled at his pipe, frantically summoned his dogs, murmured something incoherent, raised his cap, and went stamping away. After a bit he stopped, flipped up a toadstool with his stick, demolished some withered stalks of cow-parsley. He breathed deeply, saying Hmmmmmmmmmmm . . . Then he said : I'll be damned. He looked round ; but her skirts, her legs were just swinging round the corner.

Olivia went on down the path, feeling cheerful. When she got to the stile she laughed out loud, thinking what a surprise she had given him.

§ 5

There as usual were the sweep's children, or about five of the eight, hanging in a watchful breathlessly still cluster on the railings, their noses running, their dirty faces squashed against the spikes.

' Hullo ! '

' 'Allow ! '   A brief bronchial whisper, in unison.

' Been to school to-day ? '

' Yaas.'

' How's the baby ? '

Pause—

' The owld biby ? '

' Well—yes.' It certainly did seem a very old baby, pinched, bald, blue, tottering. All the same, what a queer . . . Perhaps as a term of endearment, like old chap.

' 'E's bad.'

' What's the matter with him ? '

' Got a cowld.'

' Oh dear.   And have you got colds too ? '

' Yaas.'

' All of you ? '

' Yaas.'

' You've always got colds, haven't you ? '

' Yaas.'

Pause. Their collective face was tense with more to come. They spoke.

' We got a new biby.'

' A new . . . Oh ! Have you really ? '

' Yaas. Come las' night.'

' How nice.'

' Yaas. Muvver says if they send 'er any more she'll frow 'em awiy.'

Intensely serious they were, hoarse, wary ; forlorn as a group strayed from another world and clinging defensively together. Their eyes were sharp, bright, hard, rats' eyes above high sharp cheekbones, their lips long, thin and flat, their skulls narrow and curiously knobbed. They didn't look like other people's children. They had hardly any hair ; and undersized frames with square high shoulders, almost like hunchbacks, and frail legs ; and they were enclosed in large trailing ragged coats, swathes of trouser, strange adult boots that clapped and flapped as they ran. Regularly once a year the new baby became the old baby. There seemed no warning, but there it was—another weevil, blanched, shrivelled, perfectly silent,

carried forth from the cottage triumphantly
among them for an airing, as ants convey an
egg. Each year you didn't think they'd rear it,
but they did. Tough as stonecrop it pushed
up, and joined the others on the railings. They
were the worst family in the neighbourhood.
Their cottage was unwashed, unswept, ver-
minous, littered with broken glass, broken
china, odds and ends of soap-box and bedding :
a dreadful problem. Mrs. Curtis sighed heavily,
washed her hands in lysol coming back from
visiting Mrs. Wainwright with old clothes and
good advice ; looked pained, discussing each
new arrival in lowered tones with the district
nurse. Could nothing be done ? Nothing
could be done. The Wainwrights had a lot of
family feeling. Though haggard, sagging,
crooked, with chaotic teeth and hair, Mrs.
Wainwright was by no means daunted or de-
pressed, and frequently was heard to declare
she wouldn't be without one of them. Often
of an afternoon, when not actually in the throes
of childbirth, she abandoned her unprofitable
household cares, put on a spirited hat with
feathers, and took them all for a walk. Merrily
the squeaking pram trundled, brimming with

children. It was a very high, small, spidery pram, an unique design : very likely the First Pram. The older children swarmed around it. They went at a brisk pace up the road to the woods. When they came back towards dark the pram was heavier. The little ones lay softer. Sometimes it was hen feathers, sometimes rabbit fur. . . . Mrs. Wainwright was said to be a gypsy.

Finding nothing more to say, Olivia passed on. At once they abandoned their group formation and ran to the corner of the fence. She felt their eyes like gimlets in her back. When she had gone a little way, they started to call after her.

' Livee-yer ! Livee-yer ! '

Very soon a hoarse chant arose :

> ' Livee Curtis is her nime,
> Single is her stition,
> 'Appee is the luckee man
> Who mikes the alterition.'

And cackles, rude hoots and howls pursued her until she was out of sight.

Really, it didn't do to try to be nice to the little Wainwrights.

§ 6

She came to the grove of elms and the wooden gate at the bottom of the garden. There, among wet roots and rotting leaves, were three primroses in bloom. She crouched to look at and touch them, then went on up the path into the kitchen garden. She admired the cabbage bed—its frosty sea-blues and greens, the modelling of the huge compact rosettes with their strong swelling curves and crisp-cut edges. The looser outer leaves held sparkling drops and violet shadows. She shook one, listening to its silky creak, watching the transparent water-beads slip and race like quicksilver. And these proud vital shapes were doomed to be chopped up, boiled, swallowed by humans with the utmost boredom and contempt. The very word cabbage was a joke, a term of ridicule. . . . But it was no good brooding over the sufferings, the unjust fate of vegetables. It was enough to have to worry about every thin dog, cat, horse one passed ; to be gnawed with misery for birds in cages, cattle driven to market ; to be unable to kill a wasp or squash an earwig ; to feel a twinge

78

even about flowers—in case it hurt them to be picked, torn from their companions.

Oh, how could I face it if I ever had a great sorrow. . . . Could one hope to escape?— avoid each accident by slipping round the corner? For a time perhaps; not for ever. One was just walking irrevocably onward to the places where people would die. Dad! She saw him in her mind's eye pacing slowly up and down, stopping to draw hard breaths, wrestling with his breath on bad asthma days. Oh, Dad, I'll make you all right! She flew to him, to release him from that trap, to give him back smooth inaudible breath. . . . It couldn't be done. One had to stand beside him and listen. He said smiling: Not so good to-day. He never complained more than that about it. Another five years and he'd be seventy: an old man. Mr. Curtis has aged a lot lately. People were always saying that nowadays. Damn them, damn them. Aunt Edith on her last visit murmuring to Uncle Oswald: Surely I see a great change in Charles?—hoping to whisper about it, talk it over. But Uncle Oswald, bless him, had brisked up and snapped back: Change be

hanged. Never been better. None of us get
any younger. *You* don't. He couldn't bear
his sister. . . . And anyway heaps of people
lived to be well over eighty : especially in-
valids. It wouldn't happen for a long time ;
and by then one would be different, tougher.

§ 7

She saw two figures ahead of her in the rose
garden—James and Miss Mivart, returning
from their nature walk : a melancholy sight.
The set of James's brown tweed overcoat and
cap expressed dejection. He kicked about with
his boots, throwing up leaves. From one hand
depended a meagre trail of botanical speci-
mens. Beside him stalked Miss Mivart, gaunt,
refined in black velvet toque, astrakhan bolero,
voluminous claret-coloured skirt trimmed with
rows of black braid, black goloshes : fantastic
garb, persisting year in, year out, through
summer heat and winter cold, proclaiming her
status of gentlewoman in reduced circumstances as unmistakably as did her nose the
chronic nature of her dyspepsia. Poor Miss
Mivart ; but poorer James, wretched little

sacrifice ! . . . incongruous pair yoked together
by Mother's implacable benevolence. For Miss
Mivart and her friend Miss Toomer, relics cast
up none knew whence, united none knew
why—(by some past similar chronicle, one sur-
mised, of drab reversal and disappointment,
investments mismanaged, confidence misplaced,
schemes miscarried, strokes, creeping deaths by
cancer, drain of savings)—dwelt together in a
cottage on the green, and eked out a totally
inadequate income in various painful and lady-
like ways. Miss Toomer made wholesome
sweets, Miss Mivart did pokerwork. The sweets
could be eaten with goodwill if not with relish ;
but the pokerwork class had dwindled rapidly
and was now extinct. Kate had learnt quickly
and with hostility ; Olivia had shown no
aptitude. Casting about, Mrs. Curtis saw
James, his taste for botany and Miss Mivart's
collection of pressed flowers in happy conjunction ; and forthwith James and Miss Mivart
had begun to issue forth together on Thursday
mornings. What went on inside James ? How
active was his protest, how definitely did he
know that he hated and despised Miss Mivart ?
It was plain she feared him. She told Miss

Toomer he seemed a backward child : he never spoke except to mutter such words as yes, no, oh, I don't know, good-bye . . . James was splendid, remarkable. Others besides Miss Mivart had been made uneasy by the searching appraisal of his fierce blue eyes. His strength lay in an absolute surface tractability combined with an absolute spiritual reserve and independence. She thought : I'll respect him anyway. To-night she would ask him to recite some of his poems. Soon he would be going to school ; and what would he feel about that ? No one would know. Then no longer would Miss Mivart delicately haunt the rose garden, linger in the drive after the walk, hoping to see Dad. For Dad was obviously her hero, her dream-lover, said Kate (at lunch too with Violet handing vegetables). She wore a gold locket, and Kate said it had his photo in it, the one that had mysteriously disappeared from the drawing-room one day. Nobody knew if this was true.

Olivia walked on up the garden ; stopped under the walnut tree for a quick swing ; went on over the lawn. The weather was changing somehow. The day was a different colour, a

film was gathering in the west, spreading towards the sun, tinging the light with leaden
yellow ; and the wind began to get up again,
reluctantly, as if loth to tear down the frail
and flawless texture of the morning.

§ 8

Violet met her in the hall.

' Please, Miss Livia, there's a young person
to see you.'

' To see me ? '

' Well, she wanted the one or the other of
you. Madam's out, and I couldn't find Miss
Kate. So she said she'd wait.'

' Is it one of the Miss Martins ? '

' Oh no, it's a young person. Carries a
case. I don't know what she's come after. I
showed her into the servants' 'all. Will you
see her ? '

' Yes, I suppose so.' How queer.

Violet disappeared, returned, said coldly :
Come this way, please ; and grudgingly made
way for a short slight girl of about twenty,
dressed neatly and shabbily in a fawn hat and
coat, and carrying a suit-case.

'Good morning,' she said. Her voice and smile anticipated antagonism.

She was a rather pretty anaemically pink-and-white girl with small regular features, blue circles round her eyes, and an appealing air of goodness.

Olivia said nervously :

'Do sit down.'

She sat on the edge of a chair, laid her case down, and spoke in a modest and genteel voice.

'I've brought a few things to show you—some of my work—thinking you might be interested. Are you interested in lace ?—hand-made ? ' She smiled brightly.

'I'm afraid I'm . . . I don't know anything about it.' Olivia's heart sank. She blushed deeply.

'Well, if I might just unpack my case. Real lace is so nice, I think, don't you ? It looks nice on anything. And of course it's quite a rarity these days.'

She knelt on the floor, opened her case, and began to rustle about swiftly, with tiny narrow hands, among sheets of tissue-paper.

Now was the moment to say it was no good,

that one didn't want any lace, had no money
with which to buy it. Oh, cruel fate! Any
other day that would have been true. To-day
Uncle Oswald's ten-shilling note seemed to
crackle audibly in her pocket, refusing for its
late master's sake to be denied.

Now was the moment to enquire search-
ingly into her credentials. She feebly ventured:

'Did you make it yourself?'

'Oh yes, all myself,' said the girl softly,
lightly. Clearly she was gaining confidence.
Not often could she have had such an auspi-
cious start. 'You see, I have my mother to
keep. She's a total invalid, of course—
paralysed; so not being able to go out to
work I took up lace-making. This is my
biggest piece—a bedspread.' She unfolded it,
held it up in both arms. 'It took me six
months, this did.'

'Did it really?'

And instead of coldly glancing before handing it back, one found oneself examining it,
murmuring sympathetically:

'Doesn't it tire your eyes?'

'Oh yes, they get ever so strained. That's

the worst of it. My eyes aren't strong, and if they were to give out, well, I don't know where we'd be.' She gave another bright smile. ' Of course I have my regular customers, but this time of year I go round and try to earn a bit extra, just to get Mother some little comforts for Christmas. It's for her I do it. It isn't very nice really to have to go round—you know what I mean. You feel you come at an awkward time and—it's ever such a drag and——'

' Yes, it must be.' Picture of door after door being shut in her face by haughty parlour-maids. ' How awful for your mother.'

' Yes, and she's ever so patient—never a grumble. This is a little tea-cloth. You can't have too many tea-cloths, can you? A table set—centre-piece and six mats. These little mats are all the rage now, aren't they?—so much daintier than a tablecloth. A nightdress case. Some little traycloths—they're nice. A set of doylies. . . .'

' They're beautiful. . . . But I'm rather afraid they wouldn't be quite what I . . . not very much use . . .'

' Not for Christmas presents? ' She was gently surprised.

'Well, yes, of course. Only, as a matter of fact I haven't really started to think about Christmas yet.'

'Hadn't you? I always think with Christmas shopping it's best to get it done in good time, don't you? Then it's off your mind.'

The case was nearly empty now. Olivia said suddenly, with a show of firmness:

'I believe it would be best if you could call again later—after lunch, perhaps—when my mother'll be in. I'll tell her. I'm sure she'd like to . . . She'd know better than me.'

'I'm afraid I couldn't do that.' Her voice was gentle but decided. 'I've a long way to go.'

'Yes, I suppose you have.'

She saw through that all right.

'Oh, this insertion will interest you. For trimming underwear. In different widths. Ladies always like my insertion. It's strong, yet dainty.'

'I don't wear lace on my underclothes, I'm afraid.'

'No—really?' She raised her eyebrows, politely shocked, incredulous.

' No, I don't like it.'

Firmer and firmer.   Silence fell.

' A little collar.'   She took the last package from the case and placed it upon a chair ; with hesitation, with a sudden collapse of assurance.

Silence again.   She knelt on the floor among a litter of white paper, lace and linen, her hands loosely folded in her lap, her head drooping.   Then slowly she started to fold up the bedspread, then the teacloth, the centre-piece, to smooth out the tissue-paper, to put everything back in the old suit-case ; with meek gestures, with silent disappointment folding up, laying away her unwanted handiwork.

It was too much.   Olivia picked up the collar.

' This is *very* pretty.'

The girl glanced up.

' Yes, it's a nice little collar.   It's so uncommon.'   She went on packing.

' I think I'd like . . . It would be so useful. How much is it ? '

She paused, then said :

' It's fifteen and six, that one.'

' Fifteen and six !   Oh, I'm afraid I can't,

then—I've only got ten shillings—at the
. moment.'

And quickly, for fear of being suspected
again, she drew her purse from her pocket,
opened it under the girl's nose, and extracted
its sole contents—the ten-shilling note.

' There's a lot of work in this collar. You
can see for yourself.'

' I know.' Hope sprang up again. The
miserable offer was to be rejected. ' I'm so
sorry. I can't . . .'

The girl continued reflectively :

' Still—I might make you a special price—as
you're a new customer. I'll let it go for ten
shillings.'

' Oh, will you ? Well, thank you very much.
That's splendid.'

The girl took the note, put it in a large
black handbag, thanked her politely, without
warmth, and went on packing. Suddenly she
said with decision :

' I'd have liked you to have had the tea-
cloth. You'd pay double the price for it in
any shop.'

' No, thank you, I couldn't. I'm afraid I
must go now.'

Too late, she felt all the necessary resolution.

The girl closed and strapped the suit-case, got up, lifted it with a slight effort.

' I hope it's not too heavy for you.'

' It is a bit heavy.'

And perhaps no lighter by the end of the day. . . . Dragging herself home late at night. . . . A weak voice from the pillow, whispering anxiously : Well ? . . . Brokenly answering : Only one collar. . . .

' Come out this way.'

She opened the front door. They smiled faintly at one another. The girl said with restraint :

' Thank you very much.'

' I do hope you'll be able to get plenty of— of comforts for your mother.'

' Yes. Thank you.'

Whatever they were, surely ten shillings would buy a certain amount of them.

' Good-bye.'

' Good morning.'

She went down the steps and along the drive, hobbling on irritating matchstick legs, one puny shoulder pulled down by the weight of the suit-case.

Olivia shut the door. She went upstairs, and found Kate in the schoolroom, bending over the table, her mouth full of pins, cutting out a pair of mauve georgette cami-knickers. She said sharply through the pins :

' Well, what did you decide ? '

' What about ? . . . Oh— ' The dress seemed very remote. ' Sort of draped and . . . She's going to cut the bodice on me. It's going to be lovely.' But no silver rose now.

' Hmm. You take care. Remember what she did to your velveteen. I'd better come with you. She hasn't any more idea than you have when a thing fits.'

Olivia was silent. Glancing up, Kate thought her expression sulky. Offended. So, after a bit, feeling the point must be stressed, she said kindly but firmly :

' Well, you haven't, have you ? '

' Like to see what I've bought with my ten bob ? ' cried Olivia ; and she flung down the collar upon the table.

' Good Lord, what's that ? ' Kate held it up by one corner.

' Isn't it pretty ? '

' Where on *earth*—— ? '

There was nothing for it but to tell the whole story.

' Lumme ! ' said Kate. ' So that's what that foul Violet came flouncing up here for. I hid.'

She spread the collar out upon the table and was silent, examining it.

' Don't you think it's rather nice ? '

It was looking its worst somehow : exactly as if it ought to be thrown on the fire.

' How much did she rook you ? '

' Ten bob.'

' The whole lot ? '

' Yes. She reduced it for me.'

After a pause, Kate said :

' What'll you do with it ? '

' Oh, put it on some frock, I suppose. It's bound to come in somehow. Real lace always does.'

Faintly Kate's nostrils dilated, but she said nothing. This was more bad luck than down-right folly, and she could sympathize. Yet Olivia felt her pretences snatched away, Kate's finger pointing the way inexorably to surrender, to truth. She said suddenly :

' Don't tell Mother.'

' Of course not.'

' Bang goes my whole income.'

Kate nodded, murmured :

' Sickening.'

' I'll give it to Nannie for Christmas. She'll love it.' She giggled, blinked back a tear. ' Little will she guess what I've spent on her. She'll think it came from Evans, one and eleven three.'

' Perhaps it does,' said Kate, busy with paper and pins.

' Don't be absurd. It's handmade. You can see it is. . . . Can't you ? '

' *I* don't know.'

' Well, how does one tell ? . . .'

All supports cracked together. She threw up her hands, fell.

' Do you think—' Kate spoke with unwonted hesitation—' she can have been—could it have been a swizz ? '

' Of *course* not. She was awfully sort of superior. And all that about her mother. She couldn't have made that up.'

' I suppose not,' agreed Kate, starting to cut out.

Olivia sat down and meditated upon the transaction. I never disliked any one so much,

she thought. The worst was the lack of gratitude. Ten shillings snatched by compulsion,
stuffed into her black bag, sitting there quiet
and avid as a spider, then asking for more . . .
asking for more. No, she was not pathetic. She
was sinister.

She picked up the collar and threw it into
the corner.

' It's not as bad as that,' said Kate.

Olivia yawned.

' Lord, I'm hungry ! It's been a full
morning.'

§ 9

After dining-room tea, after the pink-and-
white silver-studded birthday cake, they came
back to the schoolroom. The red curtains
were drawn. Dark, rough, thick, heavy,
faded in streaks, with a corded fringe, they
were mysterious still, and dear ; they had virtue
in them. Still, when they were drawn on
winter evenings, they distilled out of their old
serviceable folds echoes, whiffs, savours of their
old powerful life. Still, now and then they
seemed to be holding behind them the sur-

prising, the magic vistas of childhood—the
sudden snow at night, whirling and furring
without sound against the window ; the full
moon and all its shadows on the lawn ; the
Christmas sleigh and reindeer in the sky.
Sometimes, brushing against them, one saw
them move secretly, sway, and become once
more those hide-and-seek towers, wrapping the
child round in dark safety threaded with dark
fear. And still, now and always, they symbol-
ized protection ; barring out the moaning
wind and all ill-wishers of the night.

They pulled the electric light down to the
flex's fullest stretch, and the glare, unbroken
by a shallow white glass shade, poured over
their lustrous hair—Kate's blond, Olivia's
brown—and exposed only to enhance the flawless freshness of their skins. Both were sunk
in dilapidated basket chairs. Kate sewed, her
crammed basket on the hairy green tablecloth
beside her. Olivia read. The sagging wicker-
work creaked gently as they stirred.

Around them crowded the well-worn and
serviceable objects of their inheritance. A
couple of school desks stood in the window—
ink-splashed, scored with two generations of

initials, their pinewood knots decorated with
top-hats, faces, whiskers, grotesque legs and
bodies. Boys and girls had dropped ink on
the faded carpet, puppies had contributed
yellowish maps. A huge cupboard occupied
one wall, a huge bookcase another. The ponderous mantelpiece was covered with china
animals, postcards and family photographs.
Grandparents, aunts and cousins ; Mr. Curtis
as an undergraduate in a blazer, his thick locks
upstanding in a quiff, arms folded, glaring ;
Mrs. Curtis in her wedding-dress, her hair piled
up on top of her head, her waist constricted,
looking gravely over her shoulder with something of Kate's features, delicate but pro-
nounced, something of Kate's look, her soft
severity, her cold appeal—a bud of beauty
which, handed on, had flowered in her
daughter ; Kate, Olivia, and James in various
juvenile groups. On the buff walls, Dignity
and Impudence, The Monarch of the Glen,
Angel Heads, a Raphael Madonna and Child,
When Did You Last See Your Father, Hope
on the orange, hung in a row. There was also
a print of a coach arriving at an inn in a
snowstorm on Christmas Eve ; a small coloured

reproduction of the Blessed Damozel, Olivia's favourite picture, and a sprig of holly executed in water-colours by Kate.

All was shabby, hard-wearing, ill-assorted ; but the years had imposed a unity on what was intrinsically chaotic ; and the character of honest dependability pervading the room, its gradually matured emotional content (store-room that it was of generations of adolescence), had, in defiance of all standards of taste, produced an impression that stood for beauty : as beauty clings round the ample white apron, the wrinkles, the neat greying hair of an old nurse.

In a trance of voluptuous anguish, and for the fifth time, Olivia read *David Copperfield*. Her throat ached. Loudly she sniffed. She lay dead, his mother : so beautiful, so girlish, with the dead baby in her arms. Peggotty had given him her last message. And now he was alone in the world—a broken heart, helpless, misunderstood : no, worse than alone—in the relentless grip of fiends. Oh, those Murd-stones, those Murdstones ! . . . Oh, what ghastly suffering. And ghastlier to follow. Peggotty, last support, to be taken from him.

Hot tears dripped on to her jumper, on to the
page. Her nose swelled. No more, no more.
But more there must be. Read on one must.
She read on. Agony sank to mere discomfort.
Relief came. It was over. No more crises till
Dora dies.

'Enjoying yourself?' said Kate.

'Mm.' She laid down the book and blew
her nose. 'Oh dear! I wonder if I shall
howl over it just as much when I'm seventy.'
She sighed, felt suddenly cheerful. 'Let's see.'

Kate held up the cami-knickers.

'Divine. Take care Mother doesn't see.
She'd have kittens.'

'Why? She hasn't got to wear them.'

Olivia thought this funny and giggled.

'I must say I should find them draughty
myself.'

'Don't be so suburban. What do *you* pro-
pose to do for the dance? A woolly bodice
tucked in in lumps round the top? Etty wears
practically nothing in the evenings—just her
belt and knickers. She says no one *dreams* of
wearing any more.'

'Oh, I wish Etty would come and stay. . . .'

'If only we could give a dance ourselves

and get her to bring some men from London—
choose a time when the Heriots were here.
Why shouldn't we? Oh, why not? Why
should we never have any fun?'

'Never mind. Think of next week. Think
of Paris.'

Kate thought of next week. But would Tony
Heriot be there? And if so, would he ask for
a dance? These were the anxieties that wore
one down. One tried to be sensible, but really
it seemed useless to attempt to get him out of
one's head; as if the key to the whole evening,
its rapture or its misery, was in his hands.
I've got him on the brain. So stupid when
she'd only met him two or three times—in the
days when he was a schoolboy and hadn't got
so grand. The last time was at a fancy-dress
party in Tulverton, three years ago, when he
as a black pierrot and she as a Greek maiden
had danced together all the evening. She remembered him taking off his ruff, saying:
Beastly hot these things. Wish some one would
turn the jolly old hose on me; looking down
at her with candid admiration, saying: . You
don't look as if you ever sweated—excuse the
word; saying also in reply to her question,

which dress did he like best in the room?. Well, I must say I like yours as much as any. Suits you. Also he had advised her to put ammonia in her bath when she came in from hunting. It had created a very intimate atmosphere, talking like that about baths. She hadn't mentioned that she didn't hunt. His voice was cracking, and this made every sound he uttered—and especially his frequent laugh— both funny and fascinating. But he hadn't asked what her name was. And at the end he'd just said good-bye—quite airily, with a careless smile, and gone off to put his coat on without one backward look.

And this time would he even remember her? Once again, for the hundredth time, she pictured the scene. . . . Of course I haven't forgotten you. Is it likely? Why haven't we met for so long? How many can you spare me? Four? Five? I suppose you haven't any extras left? . . . Melting into the dance again and again, his arm around one's waist. Oh, bliss! . . . But one mustn't—one *must not* go on like this. It would be unlucky.

I will put my faith in prayer. More things are wrought by prayer . . . After a glance at

the unconscious Olivia she closed her eyes. . . .
Nothing direct or importunate now—no bar-
gaining ; at least, no more than could be
helped.

Lord, if Thou seest fit, all unworthy though
I am, let this happen. I am very selfish, bad-
tempered, envious and vain, coveting the things
of this world and not so content as I should be
with my lot. But shouldst Thou see fit to grant
this I will do better . . . with Thy help I will
do better henceforth and try to please Thee in
all my ways. For Jesus Christ's sake. . . .

Oh, never bad-tempered or envious again !

§ 10

Olivia went to her desk, opened it and took
out her new diary. She gnawed her pen for a
bit, then wrote :

'My seventeenth birthday. I have decided
to keep a record of my inmost real-self thoughts.
Perhaps it will help me to find out what I
really am like : horrid, I know : selfish, conceited, and material-minded. For instance,
lately whenever I've tried to concentrate on
anything serious or beautiful, I've started think-

ing instead about the Spencers' dance next week. I am ashamed of my pettiness. I'm going to try to do better this year—develop my character more and not always be thinking about enjoying myself. I've always been so happy, I dread disappointment and unhappiness, but they would be good for me. *But I don't want them.*

' In this journal I shall write out any poetry that I like—also any poem I make up. Also perhaps some of my dreams, as they really are so very extraordinary.'

She thought again for a bit ; went on :

' *David Copperfield*—what a book ! It's awful to be made so that you can't keep back your tears and cry at the least thing that moves you. I would like to sink underground or faint when I remember how I cried over Algebra last term. I couldn't understand it—I never shall—and hateful sarcastic Mr. Blenkinsop said with such cutting politeness : " Shall you never master the first principles, Miss Curtis ? Perhaps I am wasting your time." Kate cries over books too, though she is such a strong character : a much stronger one than me.

' She heard to-day from Reginald Kershaw

that he can come for the dance. He's at Oxford. I wonder what he'll be like. Kate and I have different ideas about him. We shall see.'

After a pause she wrote :

' I wonder if I shall keep this up.'

And after another pause :

' *Advice to Young Journal Keepers*. Be lenient with yourself. Conceal your worst faults, leave out your most shameful thoughts, actions and temptations. Give yourself all the good and interesting qualities you want and haven't got. If you should die young, what comfort would it be to your relatives to read the truth and have to say : It is not a pearl we have lost, but a swine?'

She locked up the diary, put it back in the desk, went to her bedroom and hid the key in the bottom of her jewel-case.

With dusk a little snow had begun to fall, and she lifted the blind and peered out to see what the night promised. To her surprise, a glistening, crumbling drift was already piled upon the ledge and a storm of big flakes came slipping and swarming giddily out of nothingness towards the pane. The hidden moon was high in the sky, and it was easy to see the hoods of snow over yew hedge and laurels, and the snow serpents in the branches of the walnut tree.

December and the first snow. Weeks, weeks, weeks of winter ahead before the lengthening days brought that kind of snowfall which seems a promise of change, of growth : as if the infant spring has cast its shawl ; which ceases with soft sunshine and a rejoicing clamour of birds, and melts soon, leaving in wet woods and gardens, among aconites, snowdrops, crocuses, frail wreaths which seem another flower.

This snow was mournful, sinister, charged with death. It was choking the last of earth's springs of life. It was the shroud.

Snow on my birthday. . . . That had never happened before. It was a certain sign of growing up that one no longer loved the snow ; no longer wished to rush out and stamp in it and throw it about. To-morrow James would toil and grunt across the lawn behind his giant snowball with only Simpkin to take a real interest.

To-morrow we'll wake up and find a white

world. That was an old nursery saying. I'll go and tell James that he's going to wake up to a white world.

She went along the passage to the night nursery, and found that he had pushed his bed up to the window and was sitting up on the pillows enveloped in the eiderdown.

'Hullo, James.'

'Hullo.'

'Shall I switch the light on?'

'If you like,' he said politely. 'I turned it out myself to see better.'

'What are you doing?'

'Looking at the snow.'

'Did you move the bed yourself?'

'Yes.'

Lost in the quilt's voluminous folds, he looked comically ceremonious, lonely, smaller than usual. She felt moved, looking at his serious, impassive face, trying to follow his mysterious actions and motives: the solitary shifting of his bed, the precaution of the eiderdown.

'To-morrow when we wake up we'll see a white white world.'

'Mm.'

He was not responsive to stock romantic

suggestions. Probably he was engaged in some prodigious mathematical calculation connected with the snowfall.   No billion or even trillion could daunt him.   There was no doubt James was going to be a genius.   Everybody said so. She felt inclined to apologize to him for interrupting.

He said :

' There was lightning a little while ago. Did you see ? '

' No.'

' And thunder. Perhaps there'll be some more.'

She felt a faint inward contraction.   These words still had power to awake an echo of fear ; like an old half-forgotten threat resuscitated, potent no longer yet ill-sounding.

' When I was a little girl I was very frightened of thunderstorms.'

' Were you ? '

' We used to pull down the blinds in the nursery and put on all the lights, and wind up the musical-box and do very loud stamping dances.'

' Did you ? You and Kate dancing ! Ha ! Ha ! How funny ! What funny girls you must have been.' He delighted in reminiscences of his sisters' early days. 'Why were you frightened? Were you ever struck?'

'No. I didn't like the noise.'

'I like the noise. I should like to see somebody struck.'

'Oh no, James, I'm sure you wouldn't.'

'Well, a tree, then. But it doesn't hurt, you know.'

'Once I thought I'd been struck. I was washing for tea in the bathroom and I saw the lightning flash all over my hands. So I rushed into the nursery with my hands all dripping and soapy, roaring: Boohoo! I've been struck, I've been struck!' She acted the scene, grimaced, flapped her hands.

'When you hadn't been at all?'

'Not at all. I just thought I had.'

He bounced on the bed in a paroxysm; radiant with delight.

'And what did Kate do?'

'She ran for Mother.'

'And what did Mother do?'

'She told me not to be so silly.'

His face fell. It seemed all too probable—an anticlimax. He was silent.

'Have you made up any poetry lately, James?'

'Yes.'

'May I hear it?'

'I did one this morning on my nature walk.'

He recited rapidly, in a monotonous singsong:

'Oh nature, oh nature, with all thy powers,
What dost thou do through the long winter hours?
I love thee, oh nature, so sweet and so good,
But where dost thou get thy winter food?'

'I like that very much.'

'You have to take care how you pronounce food, or else it doesn't rhyme. Unless you say gooood. You might do that.'

Without a pause he shot out:

'Too many things have we got to,
Too many things have we not to.

'That's another.'

'Very good indeed.'

It was really—well, it was quite startling, coming out so glib and matter-of-fact. Philosophy in a nutshell. But of course it was merely the rhyme that had attracted him. . . . Was it? Looking at his inscrutable face, one could not be certain.

' You must write them all down so that you won't forget them. I'll give you a notebook.'

' Will you ? Oh, good ! Then I can use my new Tomtit pen.'

' Nannie'll be in in a minute. Hadn't you better lie down ? '

' All right.'

She extracted him from his wrappings. He lay down with docility, and she pushed his bed back and kissed him.

' Good-night.'

' Good-night.'

As she reached the door he said suddenly :

' Did you like that present I gave you ? '

' I simply loved it.'

She was seized with guilt. What have I done with it ?

' It's in the cupboard in the hall . . . isn't it ? I saw it there.' His voice was wary but not hurt or reproachful.

' Oh yes. I put it there to keep it safe. I was so afraid it might be broken. I'm going to fetch it now this very minute and put it on my bedroom mantelpiece. You come and look to-morrow.'

Her falseness seemed to her to proclaim itself

aloud. He couldn't possibly be taken in : he would never trust her any more. But he said placidly :

'All right. Guess what it cost ? '

'An awful lot, I should think. Sixpence ? '

'Tenpence halfpenny ! '

Nor did he see through her pretence of incredulity. He beamed, he glowed with triumph.

She thought with relief that he was still a baby after all : quite transparent, quite easy to deceive.

§ 11

After supper, everybody sat in the drawing-room. The fire blazed, and the light was very bright and white, coming from three brass standard lamps with white silk shades. In front of the fire was a large white wool rug, excessively shaggy—the work of Mrs. Curtis. The carpet was pale blue and the chintz had a pattern of full-blown pink roses, green leaves and blue ribbon on a white ground. There were a number of little tables covered with ornaments and photographs, a Japanese fire-screen, an ebony cabinet crammed with china, a grand piano decorated with an Italian shawl and more photographs, and some Indian brass pots and trays which Mrs. Curtis had inherited. On the walls hung, in gilt frames, the water-colour sketches of aunts and great-aunts, including several views of the house and garden. They were very well done, and looked exactly like what they were meant to be.

Mr. Curtis wore his corduroy slippers and read the *Spectator*, glasses on nose. He breathed loudly, and from time to time was shaken by his cough, but he went on reading just the same. He sat crookedly and in a rather cramped way, out of consideration for Simpkin, who shared his chair.

Uncle Oswald folded his hands upon his paunch and went to sleep. At intervals he snorted violently, roused, fixed one or other of his nieces with a stare, nodded off again.

Kate and Olivia wore their long-sleeved velveteens—Kate's Wedgwood blue, Olivia's chestnut brown. Kate's had a square neck, Olivia's a round. Kate wore a pink crystal heart on a gold chain, and Olivia wore her ambers. They sat on the sofa and played ludo, with occasional squeals and exclamations. The dice rattled with hollow persistence, the counters tapped rapidly up and down the board. Kate said blast, and Mrs. Curtis glanced at her ; but she said nothing.

Mrs. Curtis wore, over her black dress, a black chiffon scarf embroidered with gold sequins. She knitted. To-night it was stockings for James. To-morrow night another kind of wool would be wound, another work embarked on. Now and then her hands dropped in her lap and she sighed—a long sigh, unconscious, profound ; and each time, hearing it, her daughters felt uneasy, wondering from what depth issued a symptom so contrary to her nature. For though they told themselves it was only an irritating habit, it sounded each time so terribly like the sigh of one afflicted, bearing up beneath some secret burden of knowledge : as if, though the world imagined her impregnable, she knew herself undermined ; as if, instead of sailing on majestic, invulnerable for ever, she knew she must sink soon, die, say, of heart disease ; but meanwhile she would do her duty, keep silence as long as she could, let no shadow fall upon her dear ones.

The clock struck ten. Kate won her game, got up, yawned.

' I'm going up to get a bath while the water's hot. 'Night all.'

She bent languidly to be kissed by her parents and left the room.

Half an hour later came official bedtime. Uncle Oswald was wakened, Simpkin was let out by the French windows and stood barking upon the step. Mr. Curtis put on a woollen scarf, took a small torch and vanished with him into the garden. Flashing his torch hither and thither, with mild exhortations and encouragements he skirted the length of the house ; and when Simpkin had lifted his leg three times, he praised him and brought him in again, and made him comfortable for the night in his armchair.

Not for the first time, Mrs. Curtis said :

' Charles, why don't you let one of the girls do that ? '

She received no answer.

They put out the lights and went upstairs. Outside her bedroom door, Mrs. Curtis kissed Olivia, patted her shoulder.

' Good-night, my big girl.'

Thus the dying birthday was gently breathed on, flickered up for a moment and expired.

Olivia undressed quickly, looking forward to half an hour's reading in bed. She had put on her nightdress and was brushing her hair when a white square on the pillow caught her eye : an envelope addressed to her in Kate's dashing hand. As she opened it she heard a clink of coins. She unfolded a sheet of paper and found two half-crowns. On the paper was written :

> ' We may as well share it.
> With love to an idiot.'

Oh, Kate !

A tide of emotion surged up and made her face flame.

Rush now at once and thank her. Oh, gratitude—how embarrassing. . . . What shall I say, do. . . . But quick. No shirking.

She tore along the passage and opened Kate's door. All was in darkness. She called softly.

But Kate lay quiet as a mouse, feigning sleep.

PART II

PART II

Time crawling by at length delivered up
the evening of the dance.

That morning Mrs. Curtis said :

' Nannie, you'll help the girls to dress, won't
you ? ' And they felt the first thrill of pre-
paration. It sounded so important and correct, as if they were authentic debutantes with
a maid, like Marigold, to lay out, to fold up
after them.

Upon their beds lay the dresses. Olivia's
had come home that morning from Miss Robinson with a note pinned to it. *Have a nice time.
E. Robinson.* The underclothes were prepared,
the new satin slippers, the long kid gloves
borrowed from their mother ; and Nannie,
rising superbly to the occasion, had crowned
all by running the bath for them and spreading
their towels over the chair ; so that all they
had to do, after Kate had shaken in a packet
of Heart of a Rose bath-salts, was to step in
and lie back one at each end. Even the

nursery bathroom, with its scarred white paint and old red blind, its enamel mug bristling with the family toothbrushes, its well-worn paraphernalia of sponges, face-cloths, nail-brush and pumice-stone, its cake of plain Castile soap, its faded eighteen-year-old bath-mat stencilled with animals—even the nursery bathroom seemed somehow glorified and new ; seemed to lose its true character of straight-forward scrubbing place, and, veiled in un-wonted clouds of scented steam, to take on an air of luxury and refinement, suitably en-shrining the ritual of young ladies at their toilet.

' All this extra regard for detail,' said Kate, ' and we shall look just the same in the end.'

' And smell the same.   After a bit.'

After a silence Kate said, squeezing the sponge over her shoulders :

' I shouldn't think *he'd* notice if we came down in our knickers and stank of onions.   I didn't see him look at us once—did you ?   He must be a woman-hater.'

' I expect he's awfully shy.   He hasn't got any sisters.   Did you see what long eyelashes he's got ?   Only they're so fair you don't notice

them. He isn't really bad looking—is he?—
except for the pince-nez. . . . Miss Robinson
calls them pinch-knees.'

Kate smiled, but mournfully. The glasses
had been a cruel blow ; exactly what she had
foretold in her gloomiest prognostications.

Olivia added :

' Perhaps he'll leave them off for the dance.'

Kate checked the retort which rose to her
lips, 'And go falling over everybody's feet . . .,'
and, willing for once to be seduced by Olivia's
insensate optimism, merely said in a meek and
yearning voice :

' Do you think he might ? '

She tried to dismiss from her mind the dis-
couraging scene of his arrival at five o'clock,
in a dripping wet burberry, soaked suit-case in
hand, having walked the mile from the station
after missing the village taxi painstakingly sent
by Mrs. Curtis to meet him. The first glimpse
had revealed him standing in the hall, wiping
his glasses, dabbing at his neck, at his dank
burberry-coloured hair, repeating in a loud
flat voice that it was nothing, it didn't matter,
he didn't mind a bit—stressing his plight instead of laughing at it, or even enjoying it as

a proper young man should (as Tony Heriot
would have). After that, how passionately one
had wished to return him at once, marked
Not Suitable. Perhaps, he'd said, he'd better
get out of his wet things at once, as he was
liable to colds : might he borrow some dry
clothes ? So tea had been put off half an hour
while he bathed and changed into a flannel
shirt and a pair of grey flannels from his host's
wardrobe. Then at tea, after asking him if
he went to many dances and hearing he didn't,
after saying did he like dancing and hearing
he liked it in moderation—after that there
seemed nothing to do but sit and watch him
take greedy helps of butter and honey, and
listen while he told Mrs. Curtis about the
necessity for an operation for cataract upon his
mother.

Kate and Olivia had had the melancholy
satisfaction of studying his appearance without
once being obliged to avert their eyes out of
modesty or politeness ; for he neither looked
at them nor seemed aware of their scrutiny by
so much as a twitch. He sat with his head
poking forward on a short neck between high
round shoulders. His skin was smooth, pinkish,

rather shiny—not a healthy rough shine, but a sort of surface glisten, very unappetizing. His mouth shut like the two halves of a muffin It too was shiny, rather full and pale. His eyes were opaque, the same colour as the hair on his flat broad head. He was not exactly ugly, they thought : but one might be alone with him on a desert island for ten years without ever being able to bear to kiss him.

After tea, Mrs. Curtis, with a look which said, Now, girls, you must look after your guest, went away to write letters. They took him into the drawing-room and put a ukulele solo on the gramophone. But he didn't seem to listen. Then they put on *Rustle of Spring*, in case his tastes were classical. But still he didn't seem to listen. He sat in the best arm-chair with his legs crossed, looking at the toe of his stubby black shoe and pulling rhythmically at his forelock. He appeared quite at home.

' Do you like music ? ' said Kate.

' I beg your pardon ? '

She repeated very loudly :

' Do you like music ? '

' Oh. Well, as a matter of fact I don't

particularly care for the gramophone. But do go on if you like it.'

' Oh no, I wouldn't dream of it. We know every record by heart. We were doing it entirely for you.'

She shut down the gramophone lid with a bang and shot him one of her witherers. But he didn't notice it. Then she opened the new box of Abdullas bought in his honour.

' Cigarette ? '

' Thanks, no. I don't smoke.'

Then it was six-thirty, and they gave him a bound volume of *Punch* to look at, and left him and went upstairs to dress a good half-hour earlier than necessary.

' Perhaps we ought to have suggested ludo or demon,' said Olivia on the stairs.

' It wouldn't have been any use. " Thenks, no. I don't particularly care for games." Can't you hear him ? '

Olivia giggled.

' You were naughty to say that about the gramophone.'

' Well, did you ever— ? I can't stand those priggish sort of idiots. . . . What price your clean-limbed footballer ? '

But now, after an hour's absence from him, she felt inclined to be more hopeful. At least he was a partner. Unprepossessing but not unpresentable. Perhaps he would warm up and prove a good dancer. At least he was taller than either of them ; and at least he hadn't said he'd never tried, but supposed he could walk round the room like anybody else.

They sighed, stirred idly, setting the water rippling. It was not a big bath and it looked overcrowded with their limbs. They had long well-turned arms and legs and small shapely breasts.

' Turn on the hot,' said Olivia. ' It's chilly up my end. You didn't mix it properly.'

' No. I'm getting out. So ought you. You were in before me. Look at your legs, you've simply boiled them. If you don't look out you'll come down to dinner with a lobster face again.'

She sprang up and out lightly and landed on the bath-mat. Olivia turned on the hot and lay back again.

Kate shook out talc powder (sweet geranium) all over herself in patches and rubbed it in A cloud of it rose up and veiled her.

'Lend us a spot,' murmured Olivia.

'Why can't you buy some of your own? You are so lazy, you never will think for yourself. You don't want to go through life copycatting me, do you? Didn't you read that article in the *Daily Mirror* about choosing scents and colours to suit your personality?'

Olivia said meekly:

'Yes. But I hadn't a bean in the wide after going that bust over the decoration.'

'Hmm. You'd better let me arrange that for you.'

'No thanks, bossy. I'm quite capable of sticking a flower in my own belt.'

'Hmm. Are you?'

Kate drew the cami-knickers over her slender thighs and hips. She had finished off the garment with *diamanté* shoulder-straps and a couple of pale blue butterflies *appliqué* on the legs.

'Oh! You look exactly like some one in that French paper Etty brought—what was it?— *La Vie Parisienne*. What a pity you can't go like that. You really look your best.'

Kate surveyed herself placidly.

'Wouldn't you love to see his face?' She

held out her arms and tripped forward, entreating in a tender languishing voice : ' Dance with me, Reggie. . . .'

Olivia giggled.

Kate squeezed out a double allowance of toothpaste and vigorously attacked her teeth.

' I say, you are going it,' said Olivia, still prostrate in the water.

' A young girl should be spotlessly pure both within and without.'

A sudden resolve to do likewise spurred Olivia to heave herself out and wrap herself in a towel. Then she sat down on the edge of the bath.

Kate studied her face in the mirror-front of the little medicine cupboard on the wall.

' I'm glad I washed my hair when I did. The wave's just right.' She examined her eyelashes and sighed. ' That Lashalene's a swindle. They haven't grown a millionth of an inch. None of these hush-hush things you send a postal order for ever work. Etty knew a girl afflicted with chronic red nose, and she saw an advertisement saying a lady well known in society guaranteed a cure on receipt of five bob. So she sent off the five bob, and what do you think she got ? A typewritten slip of paper saying *Drink till it's blue.* . . . Livia, do pull yourself together. It's fearfully bad for your skin to sit and soak like that, and then not dry properly.'

She whisked on her dressing-gown and vanished.

Left alone, Olivia started suddenly to life, dried, powdered, brushed her teeth. She looked at her nails : they were clean, but that was all. Kate had spent an hour manicuring hers. All these dainty devices, so natural to Kate, seemed when she performed them to become unreal, like a lesson learnt by heart, but not properly understood. Something in her fumbled, felt inharmonious, wanted almost to resist.

She experienced a sudden distress of spirit, thinking in a half-conscious way that she hadn't—hadn't yet found herself . . . couldn't— *could* not put herself together, all of a piece. During a period of insanity she had accepted, with alacrity, with excitement, an invitation to a dance. Now, this moment having re-covered her wits, she saw what she was in for.

Why go ? It was unthinkable. Why suffer

so much ? Wrenched from one's founda-
tions ; neglected, ignored, curiously stared at ;
partnerless, watching Kate move serenely from
partner to partner, pretending not to watch ;
pretending not to see one's hostess wondering :
must she do something about one again ?—(but
really one couldn't go on and on introducing
these people) ; pretending not to care ; slipping
off to the ladies' cloakroom, fiddling with un-
necessary pins and powder, ears strained for
the music to stop ; wandering forth again to
stand by oneself against the wall, hope struggling with despair beneath a mask of smiling
indifference. . . . The band strikes up again,
the first couple link and glide away. Kate sails
past once more. . . . Back to the cloakroom,
the pins, the cold scrutiny or (worse) the
pitying small talk of the attendant maid.

Oh, horrible images ! Solitude in the midst
of crowds ! Feast from which, sole non-par-
ticipator, one would return empty !

She thought of a children's party at the
Spencers', years ago ; of falling in love at first
sight with a most beautiful boy of ten called
Archie, a cousin of the house. Dancing the
baby polka with him, she had gazed enraptured

at his profuse yellow locks and angelic pale-
blue eyes. Between each dance he took a
large broom from the corner of the room where
he kept it, and swept the floor. (Why had he
done that ?) The fourth time she asked him
to dance, he replied in a ringing treble, most
gaily, most politely, rushing with his broom
down the middle of the floor : 'Another ? oh,
right you are ! We've had quite a lot of
dances together, haven't we ? ' And all the
grown-ups sitting round the room had burst
out laughing ; and the sound was like houses
falling. That had been the beginning of self-
consciousness, of failure of confidence. Some
day I'll write a story about it.

She put on her stockings, regretting their
cotton tops. With care they wouldn't show.
All the same, lisle-thread knees made absolute
poise impossible. How did Kate manage
always to have in reserve an all-silk pair ?
Kate said it was a good maxim never to go
out without making sure one would be, in the
event of accident, the body of a well-dressed
woman.

Now, how much, how little in the way of
underclothes. . . . She put on three layers,

then took off one. Even so there seemed a lack of suppleness, a thick look. Oh, for Kate's skill to fashion a featherweight trifle, her courage to wear it.

' What's that ? ' Mother had held it up between finger and thumb. ' A handkerchief ? '

' No.' Kate snatched it back, smiling a little. ' Guess again.'

Mother had guessed long ago. From the ensuing scene Kate emerged unshaken—though she whistled for a bit afterwards—flouting the categorical *I forbid* and amused at the charge of indecency.

She gathered up her discarded clothes and went back to her room. There on the bed lay the red frock, smooth, inviting, brilliant ; pressed out by Nannie, not yet tried on.

Now for the hair. She had practised nightly for the past week : this was its public debut. Part it in the middle, bring the two lots forward, plait them, coil one round each ear, like a German girl. Kate's idea. To-night the divided strands obeyed her, weaving themselves swiftly, smoothly. Round went the coils, exactly symmetrical, the ends tucked themselves neatly in. Now clamp them to the head

with dozens and dozens of pins, fortify them
with prongs. It was done. It was firm as a
rock. Not even lancers could prevail against
it. She dropped her hands and stared into
the mirror.

Yes, it suits me. Head a good shape from
the side ; and it looked nice in the place just
below the ear, where jawbone swept up in a
soft clear curve and met the neck. One single
hair was pulling somewhere out of reach. It
must just be borne. Mademoiselle, jabbing at
tangles with the comb, used to say, *Il faut
souffrir pour être belle*.

Now for the dress.

After all, I shall probably enjoy the dance
frightfully.

Quarter of an hour passed.

Kate put her head round the door.

' Ready ? '

Olivia was standing still, with leaden stillness, before the glass. One glance, and Kate
had spotted disaster.

' Here. You've got it twisted.' She gave a
few sharp twitches to the waist and skirt.
After a pause she said with restraint :

' It looks all right. Very nice.'

But it was not so. In the silence the truth weighed, became a stone that could not be rolled away.

Uneven hem ; armholes too tight ; and the draping—when Olivia looked at the clumsy lumpish pointless draping a terrible boiling-up, a painful constriction from chest to forehead started to scorch and suffocate her.

' It simply doesn't fit anywhere. . . .' The words burst from her chokingly. ' It's the most ghastly—— It's no good. I won't go looking like a freak. I must simply *rip* it off and burn it and not go to the dance, that's all.' She clutched wildly at the bodice, as if to wrench it from her.

Kate cried suddenly :

' You've got it on back to front ! '

Olivia's hands dropped.

' Have I ? ' she said meekly.

' You would.' With the asperity of relief Kate seized and reversed her hurriedly, plunged her once more through the armholes. ' Now let's see you. Hm. It drops at the back now, of course.'

Olivia turned away from the glass while Kate hooked, tweaked, patted her into shape.

It was a comfort to look into space for a little while before having to face once more the now irrevocable and perhaps scarcely improved image.

'The arms seem to catch a bit.' She crooked her elbows, strained at the seams and heard them crack with satisfaction.

'You're *not* to do that, Livia. You'll just have to bear it. Why on earth couldn't you *force* her to cut them properly? It's always the same with your clothes. You never could control her.'

'I know. I seem to make her feel so cheerful.'

Olivia sighed, thinking how at each fitting Miss Robinson had become increasingly volatile—her scissors more profuse and inconsequent, her piano-playing more frequent.

'She's loopy,' said Kate vigorously; adding, as she gave the skirt a final tweak: 'And I really believe you are too. Not to know your back from your front. How'll you ever get on in the world? Mm? . . . There.'

Now I must look.

She looked.

It was not so bad. It dipped at the back;

and there was a queer place in the waist where, owing to a mistake in the cutting, Miss Robinson had had, in her own words, to contrive it. But still, but still . . . if one didn't look too closely, it was all right. Certainly the colour was becoming.

Delivered from despair, once more a young girl dressed for her first dance—not a caricature of one—able again to compete with and appreciate others, she saw Kate suddenly with seeing eyes and cried enthusiastically :

' Oh ! You look simply topping ! '

The airy apple-green frock which Kate had made for herself flared out below her hips and clung lightly to waist and breast. A little floating cape was attached just over each flat delicately-moulded shoulder-blade by a band of minute flowers, buds, leaves of all colours. She wore green stockings and silver shoes. Against the green, her skin looked white as coral, and her hair had a green-blonde gleam.

' You look like the girl on the cover of a Special Spring Number.'

Twisting to look at her cape, Kate said placidly :

' I just took it straight from *Vogue*.'

133

Side by side they stood and looked at their reflections. After a bit Kate said :

'Thank heaven, anyway, we don't look alike.'

Olivia ventured :

'We set each other off really rather well, don't you think ? ' She thought : The younger girl, with her gypsy colouring, afforded a rich foil to her sister's fair beauty.

'Your hair's gone up all right,' murmured Kate dreamily.

'It makes me rather deaf, though.'

Kate roused herself, said briskly, 'I must go and hook up Mother,' and disappeared.

Olivia took from a drawer a silver tinsel spray—a water-lily with some leaves—and stuck it in her belt, just where Miss Robinson's graceful bow overlooped itself. From the back of the same drawer she extracted a box of powder and, breaking into its crumbling virgin surface with a swansdown puff, dabbed at her chin. The powder was pink. It took off the shine nicely, but seemed scarcely to blend with her skin. She wiped some of it off again. Would Mother notice ; and, if so, attack in public ?

Now for the crowning touch : a little scent

on the hair, for one's partners to sniff up rap-
turously. The idea came from the *Daily Mirror*
serial, whose heroine had hair smelling naturally of violets. This was one better : lily of
the valley. She opened the tiny flask—a birthday present from Nannie—and shook it into
her parting. Immediately she was drenched
in a thick sweetish yet acrid odour. It didn't
seem to smell quite like lilies of the valley,
particularly blent, as it now was, with the
smell of hair. Well, well. . . . Two hours yet
in which to become faint yet delicious. Still,
perhaps . . .

She opened the window and hung her head
out into the breeze for some minutes.

§ 2

At the turn of the passage Uncle Oswald's
door opened. Out he stepped silently beside
her.

'Hullo, Uncle Oswald. . . .'

He looked at her blankly, and she noticed
how dull his eyes were, oily. . . . There
was something about the expression on his
face, about the way he came out of his

dark bedroom softly, alone, on torn, misshapen old leather slippers, his lifeless hair
brushed neatly for dinner—something that
startled her . . . as if, taken off his guard, he
had suddenly presented to her the truth about
him.   But, though it struck heavily at her
heart, she could not quite interpret it.   Next
moment his eyes flickered ; he smiled.

' A*ha* ! '   He looked her up and down.   She
heard his paunchy breathing.

' Oh . . . Do you like it ?   I——'   She put
a hand up to her plaits, looked down, feeling
the blush begin.

' Charming,' he whispered.   ' *Siebzehn Jahre
alt* !   Going to her first ball.   Ah ! '

She said agitatedly :

' Oh . . . I'm all wrong—I know I am. . . .'

She sighed deeply.   Once more she felt the
stuff cutting into her armpits, the thin nagging
pull of her hair, the suppressed feeling of un-
suitability.   And now once more the evening
seemed threatened.   She burst out :

' I simply can't get right.   I don't know . . .'

What am I saying—to him of all people ?
Helplessly she stared into his unknown, his
familiar face.

He whispered, nodding rapidly :

'Never mind. You must just wait. Say another ten years.'

'Ten years ? '

'About that.'

'Oh . . . But I'll be old. Twenty-seven.'

'Say thirty. You'll be all right then.'

She cried out protestingly :

'Oh, what a long time ! '

The shadow of a smile ran over his face.

'You won't find it so. It goes extraordinarily quickly—even the worst of it. And really it can be—very upsetting—very upsetting indeed.' He stopped ; then said slowly, in a different voice—a voice with emotion in it, that she had never heard before : 'But it all quiets down. Yes. It gets better. Don't worry. You'll be all right in the end. I should think.'

He searched her face.

She started, at random, to deflect his scrutiny :

'The trouble is—how does one ever know . . .'

He waited, fingering his watch-chain. She stumbled on.

'I mean—Kate says you ought to know at

once—I mean, what's right and what's wrong. But I don't. Sometimes it seems as if those words hadn't any meaning. I must be unmoral. I get awfully worried. . . .'

She thought, in despair : I've gone too far, much too far. I can never get back.

He said more quietly, but still in his new, human voice :

'You needn't. You're all right. Only I suppose it may mean—you'll want what other people tell you you ought to want. Eh? Believe all you're told. You're pretty soft, aren't you? The unselfish one?'

She stammered :

'I don't know. Am I? I didn't think I was.' Her face flamed.

'Never mind,' he said gently, after a pause. 'You'll manage. But you beware of them. If you don't know what's right there's plenty who do. And they'll tell you. From the highest motives—and all in your interest. Because they know best.' Excitement had crept into his speech. He stopped, his lip twisting ; then added, more or less in his usual manner : 'At least it was so in my young days. I suppose it still is.'

She stood silent. Almost he had turned into a proper uncle, wise, kindly, giving good advice. Almost, not quite. There was nothing avuncular in the mood behind his words. She was frightened, seeing dark vistas open out before her. Twenty-seven, thirty. Why, youth would be gone. It was unimaginable. What did he mean ? In spite of the obscure and ambiguous twist of his speech, she felt his meaning crouching in it ; a prophecy of change, of mistakes, of being lonely and not happy, too much to bear. She said, to propitiate him :

' You do—sort of understand people, don't you, Uncle Oswald ? '

' Not at all. Not at all.' He held up his fat little paw.

She faltered :

' Did you feel like—me, once—then, Uncle Oswald ? ' But this he affected not to hear. He took out his watch and looked at it ; and without another glance at her, went trotting round the corner towards the stairs.

Some time, later, I'll think about this. It will seem important, extraordinary, upsetting. No time now. I'm going to a dance. Let's forget it.

She heard James call ' Girls ! Girls ! ' from the night nursery, she saw Kate come from their mother's room, angelically serene and bright, to open his door ; and she fled out from the dim passage to join them, as if from beneath the shadow of a danger back into safety.

§ 3

James was sitting up in bed doing his knitting. It was a scarlet wool comforter, a Christmas gift for his father. About a foot in length, it was dwindling rapidly now from row to row ; and there was a curious hump in the middle. He laid it down on his bedside chair, on top of the current number of *The Rainbow*, and said :

' Now, let's see you.'

Cupping his cheeks in his hands he leaned forward and eyed them piercingly.

' Do we look nice ? '

' Do you like our frocks ? '

They danced before him, pirouetting, sweeping curtseys.

' I like Livia's colour best. I like red. But I like Kate's dress best. And her shoes.'

'You think we'll do, then?' said Kate, parading like a mannequin. 'Really and truly now, don't you think we're quite the prettiest girls you know?'

'I don't know any others. Ha! Ha! Ha!' He burst into a peal of laughter. When he had got over the joke he added gravely: 'Nannie says you're not going to have breakfast till ten o'clock to-morrow.'

'No, not till ten o'clock.'

'I say, won't you be hungry! What'll you do till then? I shall be out in the garden riding my bicycle at ten o'clock.' He saw himself career madly past the dining-room window. They would watch him turn the difficult corner without falling off. 'Will that man still be here?'

'Yes.'

'Why is he going to dance with you?'

'Because he's luckier than we are,' said Kate.

'He likes dancing with girls in moderation.'

'How do you know?'

'I went in after you'd gone up and asked him, and he told me.'

'Hmm.' Kate's lips tightened, her nostrils

dilated. 'I'll moderate him.' She brooded darkly.

The gong sounded, and they started and bent down in a hurry to kiss him.

Seeing them whirl away from him in a bright soft unfamiliar flurry, he raised himself in bed and shouted after them :

' YES—YOU—ARE ! . . .'

' Are what ? '

They stopped at the door, hovering, laughing back at him. But now he was dumb.

There was no time to wait, they were gone.

He flopped down, put his head under the bedclothes and whispered :

' Pretty.'

§ 4

Dinner was over, they were back in the drawing-room. Half an hour to be got through before one could hope to hear Walker's taxi come chugging up the drive, and gracefully rise to assume one's cloak.

Dinner had gone off with every mark of refinement. There had been candles on the table under hand-painted floral shades, chocolates in little silver dishes ; the best dinner

service, *croûtons* in the creaming potato soup,
roast pheasant, a trifle liberally strewn with
cherries, angelica and whipped cream, and
definitely tasting of sherry. Mrs. Curtis was
stately in black velvet with transparent black
chiffon sleeves, her diamond necklace and
several rings in old-fashioned settings. And
though Mr. Curtis had unfortunately not
thought fit to change out of his dark grey
tweed suit, he had behaved quite impressively,
offering white wine or whisky and soda, cir-
culating the port. He had said nothing queer
at all, scarcely mentioning Simpkin, confining
himself chiefly to questions about Oxford,
addressing their guest as Kershaw. Only, as
the meal wore on, he seemed a little out of
spirits : that was all.

And though completely silent, Uncle Oswald
had, after two glasses of wine and two of port,
begun to smile a good deal in a pleasant way,
and when Mrs. Curtis rose after coffee, had
hastened forward to open the door for her.
And though he had tripped over the rug, his
old-world courtesy, his deep bow as they passed
out, had been almost as much a pleasure as a
surprise.

It was obvious to the girls how painstakingly their elders had striven to make of it a little occasion for their sakes. Dresses, coiffures had been admired ; Mother had checked her hand as it sprang to brush the powder from their noses ; Father had given them each half a glass of port and then drunk their health. Yet something was amiss. There was a vacuum in the centre where fullness was required, contraction where should have been release. Reggie quaffed his wine, took second helps of pheasant and pudding, related several long anecdotes, was perfectly at ease ; but nothing burgeoned where he trod ; and all their festive impulses turned back upon themselves and withered at the touch of his sterility.

The gentlemen had not lingered at the table. Rising precipitately when his wife rose, Mr. Curtis made off in a hurry to the smoking-room, the set of his back proclaiming a determination to wash his hands, now, of the whole thing. What was done was done ; and it was for the sake of the girls ; but it had been sheer waste and folly to open a bottle of his best port for such as Kershaw. What on earth was Ethel . . . why in the name of . . . Was the house to be infested from now on by self-important nincompoops in the guise of partners? In his day a girl didn't have to lead a man about after her in order to ensure being danced with. In any case, if they must make themselves cheap, let them at least choose—something different—proper young chaps—men. This was not at all the sort of young chap Sir John would take to.

He continued to think about his daughters in a worried way for twenty minutes. Undoubtedly they were growing up—pretty girls too. . . . Some undesirable or other would come along and want to marry them. Well, he hadn't any money to give them—none. . . . Must speak to Ethel.

They sat in the drawing-room, the girls on the fender-stool, Mrs. Curtis upright on the sofa with her knitting, Reggie lying back very comfortably in the best armchair, knees crossed, waggling one shoe, pulling rhythmically at his forelock. His voice pounded on, monotonous, flat, while he gave Mrs. Curtis a full account of a walking tour in Wales, including mileage per day, names of all places visited and inns stayed in, with notes on the

Welsh language. The wine flowed warmly through his veins. He felt he was doing himself justice. Sensible woman, Mrs. Curtis.

After the resources of Wales had been exhausted, Mrs. Curtis said graciously :

' And have you decided on a career, Reggie ? '

There was a pause ; after which he said loudly :

' I have decided to take Holy Orders.'

Mrs. Curtis counted some stitches. Then she said in a careful voice :

' That is a very fine decision.'

Silence. He said :

' My mother is very pleased.'

' I feel sure she must be.'

Silence again. The girls bent a stunned gaze upon the carpet.

Now they understood why he would not look at them. He was avoiding temptation. Neither Kate's eye, the clear, proud, challenging eye of a beauty, nor Olivia's, melting and sympathetic, should swerve him from godly thoughts, from his decision to take Holy Orders. Now they saw why he was moderate in his dancing : detached from worldly pleasures, yet in his tolerance not altogether spurning them, he

146

would be with but not of the revellers. And
oh ! they thought with sinking hearts, through
the ensuing hours, while circumspectly, moder-
ately he ambled with them through the dance,
what could they say to him now, or he to
them ? No use, thought Olivia, trying to win
him with earnest questions and rapt pure looks,
as of one secretly in tune with the infinite :
he wouldn't respond ; and anyway he was
too boring. But for Kate the position was
far worse : Kate was devout and now must
respect his future cloth, instead of putting him
in his place. He had had a Call : was above
instead of far beneath her. . . . Of course, as
Mother said, it was a very fine decision. . . .
No, it wasn't ; it was a half-witted, infuriating
decision. Just our luck, just what would
happen. . . . How Etty would laugh if she
knew. . . . Taking a curate to one's first
dance.

Now they saw him completed, fixed in an
alien firmament—dog collar, shovel hat, black
suit and all. Now they relinquished him entirely, switched off the last feeble thread of
current still hopefully flowing towards him,
swept him so finally away that when they ran

upstairs for their cloaks they did not even exchange comments upon the disaster. He was no more now than an object which must accompany them. Already they had started to look ahead, into the unknown, far, far from him, or anything he might contribute.

They washed their hands, touched their hair, filled up their evening-bags. A powder-puff in a green chiffon handkerchief went into Kate's ; and into Olivia's a dozen extra hair-pins. Each wore a voluminous wrap taken from the camphored recesses of their mother's wardrobe—Kate an embroidered blue man-darin coat, Olivia a black velvet one. Nannie came out from the nursery to whisper loudly down the passage : ' Have a nice time ! ' The cook (twenty years with the family) lumbered up the back stairs to have a look at them. And then they went down again.

' My inside's turned to water,' murmured Olivia on the stairs.

' Sh ! be quiet. Don't think about it.'

Reggie was standing by the front door. As they came towards him, side by side, faintly smiling, profoundly serious, he glanced once at them. He stood with his hands in his pockets, alien, pompous, far from youth and gaiety. As his slightly prominent eyes, eyes like marbles, rested opaquely, incuriously on them, the look he had worn all the evening did not alter. It was all one to him, the look said. He could make himself at home anywhere, take it all in his stride. If these young women desired his escort, they might as well have it.

They ran to say good-night to their father. He kissed them with affection. Pretty young creatures. He was not satisfied. All at once they seemed to him for some reason exposed, in need of protection.

'You'll find cocoa in the thermos on the hall table,' said Mrs. Curtis. 'And the biscuits. The key will be under the mat. Remember to lock up again. And put out all the lights. I shouldn't stay much after one. Good-night, Reggie.' She shook hands with him, glancing aside as she did so, so that they saw she didn't like him either. She put an arm round each of them, saying encouragingly : 'Enjoy yourselves, now. I shall want to hear all about it. And remember me very kindly to Lady Spencer.'

In speaking these last words, she adopted a special tone, remarkably affable and formal : for she and Lady Spencer were fellow-members of many a board and committee, and delicately flavoured the official with the personal in their social exchanges.

They went out into the damp and starless night, walking gingerly in their new slippers. Then the smell, sour, thick, of Walker's taxi enveloped them in its familiar exciting prelude. His hairy tickling rug was tucked around them, the little light in the roof was switched off.

At the last moment they saw their mother fly out into the dark like a wraith, crying to Walker to be careful on the bad corner.

For the next half-hour there was nothing to look at except Walker's burly unmoving silhouette, faintly illumined by the dashboard lamp ; nothing to do but listen while Reggie told them about his mother's second-hand Morris-Cowley.

PART III

PART III

From the sanctuary of the bedroom, from thick rugs, whispering voices, soft lights and mirrors, four-poster strewn with wraps of velvet, fur, brocade, they emerged—crying in their hearts : Wait ! Wait !—wishing to draw back, to hide ; wishing to plunge on quickly now, quickly, and be lost, be mingled. Mistrustfully they passed a group of unknown girls laughing together on the landing. Downstairs they went, holding the banister, dropping further and further into the giddy dimensions of the hall. A pair of enormous pewter chandeliers hung from the ceiling. The parquet floor stretched out like yellow ice, interminably. Round the base of the heavy greenish marble pillars tall chrysanthemums bulged snow-white, larger than life-size, in their tubs, among varieties of greenery and the flaring curved scimitar-petals of poinsettia. Fresh arrivals came pouring in from the outer hall, swiftly controlled and conducted as sex demanded by darting, glistening young footmen—green lizards with gilt button scales.

Uncritically their confused eyes received height, breadth, polish, profusion of flowers, and blended them into a setting of dream-like grandeur through which they walked alone— strange echoes, muffled footsteps, fleeting figures round them. But reality came back at the sight of Reggie standing beneath some mounted skulls and antlers, hands in pockets, examining them with a bland appraising air, as of a connoisseur in big game. His dress suit did not fit him at all well. Everything seemed to sag. Perhaps it had belonged to his late father. His gloves also were a good deal too big : rather like clowns' gloves. He joined them unconcernedly, and falling into the stream ahead of them they reached an open door. They saw Sir John and Lady Spencer standing by the fireplace in a room crowded with furniture, screens, glass and china ornaments, rugs and flowers. Beyond was the ballroom, brilliantly lit. In considerable embarrassment they confided their names and that of Mr. Kershaw to the butler ; were announced ; and summoning their smiles, advanced.

Lady Spencer was handsomer even than Queen Mary, in the same sculptural style, but of a more classical cast of features. A gown of silver brocade moulded her opulent but well-controlled contours ; a parure of diamonds and sapphires set off the imposing architecture of her bosom, and a tiara flashed above the severely carved wings of her grey hair. The girls adored her for her sober splendour, for the sense of lofty moral principle, of masterful beneficence, of affectionate despotism which she diffused. They feared her for her eye, hawk-sharp to spot such details of appearance and behaviour as displeased her ; for her tongue, unsparing to denounce offenders. She was always right. She knew it. They wished for her approval, and so far had retained it. She now beamed upon them, saying in her strong warm ringing voice :

' So glad to see you, my dears. How nice you look. Jack, these are Mr. Curtis's girls—you remember ? '

' Mm ? Ha. . . . Yes, of course. How de do ? '

Sir John wrung them by the hand. His expression was to some extent veiled by a heavy

moustache. Nevertheless a look of mild benevolence was apparent, blent with a kind of
gratified amusement, not unlike that which a
mastiff assumes during the investigation of a
puppy.

'We brought Mr. Kershaw,' said Kate, in a
small, smiling voice.

'How do you do? So glad to see you.'

Lady Spencer looked him over rapidly.
Commonplace; but not flashy. Clean finger-
nails. Only son—country parsonage? Bad
manner. But steady. Heavy look. Stoop—
(scholar's?). You never knew. He'd do. She
dismissed him for ever.

'Do go on through, Kate dear, Olivia. . . .
You'll find Marigold. I must introduce . . .
Rollo came down at the last moment with a
whole batch of brother officers. So we're well
off for young men. But I expect you'll find
lots of friends. . . . Oh, Mrs. Bailey, *so* glad
you could come . . . *and* Mr. Bailey.'

She had turned from them. Cast from her
protecting side, they drifted on apprehensively
and came to a halt just inside the ballroom.
The band had just stopped. Groups, including
several young men in hunting-coats, stood about

the room. And there was Marigold, running towards them, swinging a little basket full of programmes with silk cords and tiny pencils of different colours, wearing an extraordinary and fascinating frock of deep cream spotted net reaching to her ankles, high-waisted, with little puffed sleeves and rows and rows of frills round the skirt, and a sash of water-green satin tied at the back in a fly-away bow. A frock that made other frocks insipid, commonplace, unenterprising. She wore a wreath of green leaves in her fair curly hair ; and her face, that sketch in a few lines, was to-night lightly accentuated by the colours of her excitement— the blurred rose on her cheekbones, the deeper blue of her eyes, the black of their dilated pupils.

'Hullo !' Her voice was pitched high, un-like her mother's, but it had the same pene-trating ring. 'Have a programme.' She shook her basket, and all the pink, blue, green, and yellow pencils jumped and twisted on their cords. 'Here—green for Kate, yellow for Olivia. How are you enjoying yourselves ? Isn't it fun ? Rollo's come. Isn't it gorgeous ? '

They agreed enthusiastically, looking with

diffidence towards the piano, over which her brother leaned in the midst of a laughing group, strumming with one finger and joking with the pianist. Rollo was not for them.

' What a divine frock, Marigold ! '

' Oh, do you like it ? My godmother sent it from Paris. I don't feel quite myself in all this fresh white girlish muslin. I feel I ought to hang my head and sniff a daisy. Still, if you've got elephant's legs you may as well hide them.'

' You haven't got elephant's legs.'

' Oh, I *have*.' She lifted her skirt and displayed them to the knee. They were straight and sturdy, perhaps a trifle on the thick side. ' Simply enormous. Like Mum's. It's ghastly having to go through life remembering to keep them inconspicious.'

Her vocabulary, like the rest of her, was freakish, vague, gallant and capricious. Education, directed by Lady Spencer with due regard for the beauties of her mother tongue, had familiarized her with numbers of long words, but not altogether with their meaning, spelling and pronunciation. And now that education had done its worst and was behind her, they would remain her own, a surprise, a mystification and a pleasure, like the rest of her, as long as she lived.

Once more Kate ventured :

' This is Mr. Kershaw.'

' Hullo ! Have a programme.'

It seemed a waste to give him such a smile. But she did not disdain even the least of men. Free from the snobbery of physical appearance, she was ready to like them all.

' May I have a dance ? ' said Reggie abruptly.

The girls heard and observed him with surprise. He looked different. His heavy smugness had given place to an expression of goggling tenacity of purpose. In two minutes Marigold had succeeded where they had failed. He had forgotten Holy Orders.

' Love to ! ' she cried cheerfully. ' Only the bother is I'm so full up already.' She examined her programme. ' Booked till the third extra. How sickening ! '

Her long swimming eyes gazed up at him with a wistful intensity due to short sight.

Reggie said doggedly :

' The fourth extra, then.'

'Oh, right you are! Love to! Hope it isn't God Savers! . . . Let's see, what's your name? Never mind. Names are such a bore. I'll remember.'

She scrawled two words indecipherably on her programme. The words were: billiard ball.

He wrote down 'Miss Marigold Spencer,' in his meticulous hand, and put the programme in his pocket. They felt perturbed. Perhaps he thought it was enough to have dined with them, escorted them here—now he could look elsewhere, be more ambitious. . . . Not that they wanted his services. . . . Only the room seemed full of strangers. Twenty-three dances before the fourth extra. Twenty-three blanks for them. They'd have to stay to the very end now. He would certainly resent any suggestion of departure before compassing his objective.

'Oh, there's the what-d'you-call-'ems? I must fly. Are you all right for partners? You're sure to be. If not, let me know. Rollo's come. Did I tell you? Have you seen him? Do dance with him. He'll be so bored only knowing the house-party.'

She waved a hand and ran away, her airy skirts flying out round her, running like an excited child to her party.

As they watched her vanish, their smiles froze painfully. They were watching her run away from them, out of their lives, heedlessly, away from shared classes, away from asking them to schoolroom tea, from mutual jokes and confidences, from all the happy boredom, the busy emptiness, the melancholy, dreaming happiness of their common adolescence, to a world where they could not follow her. The friends she flew to join now were not their friends. They were those who would tread with her the prosperous, mapped road of coming out, whose mysteries and allurements were to be the natural setting of their days and nights. Do dance with Rollo! . . . Rollo superb in his pink coat, tall, ruddy, chestnut-haired, commanding, surrounded by his companions, every inch the only son of the house. . . . But one let oneself be beguiled. She spoke with such cordial persuasiveness, such seeming sincerity—her smiling face a mask in whose composition angelic candour mingled enigmatically with some other quality that

seemed its opposite : seemed perhaps the very
soul of falseness.

The band burst into a fox-trot. Several
couples moved out into the room and began
to dance. They must belong to the house-
party. Not noticeably lovely or well-dressed.
More or less alike they looked—fairish, pretty-
ish, of medium height, plump to thinnish, all
in the same kind of pale-coloured frock, their
hair parted at the side and waved in the same
boring kind of wave. All but one. She came
in alone by the further door, and they caught
sight of her for a moment standing beside
Rollo, nearly as tall as he, a narrow, high-
shouldered figure sheathed in white satin,
fragile neck lifting the small and shapely head
in a long curve ; black hair parted in the
middle, taken back close behind the ears and
coiled low on her neck in a heavy silky knot.
Her face turned slowly, looking round the
room. They thought they saw a face of
improbable beauty, pale, modelled in planes
never before thought of. A new face. She
turned away again, disappearing with Rollo
through the doorway.

They backed against the wall and stood side

by side, watching the revolving couples with
bright strained expressions of interest. They
could not part until some one came to part
them ; but they felt they hated one another.
Reggie stood a little apart from them, looking
at the dancers with the same air of bland
appraisal. The band went on playing and he
went on looking. At last he threw out a
casual arm, encircling the waist of the one
nearer to him, and said, gazing over her head :

‘ Want to dance ? ’

It was Olivia. Relieved, distressed, blushing, careful to avoid her sister’s eye, she placed
herself within his loose uncompromising grasp.
He launched out with her into a sober pacing.
And it was Kate who was left alone.

§ 2

For a moment she was seized by a corroding
pain.

But there was Mr. Campbell, Sir John’s
agent, a prepossessing bachelor of early middle
age, advancing towards her. Numbers 6 and
15 were booked. And immediately afterwards
came Dr. Parkes, Tulverton’s pet new up-to-

date young doctor, married, but scarcely the less interesting for that, his wife being a plain quiet girl of the home-making type, such a help to him in his profession, and—which was really so much more satisfactory—seldom accompanying him to functions owing to domestic ties : one bonny baby in the cradle, another on the way. He had attended Kate's tonsilitis last spring, and the daily appearance of his clear-cut hygienic features, compelling cold surgical blue eye, fresh complexion, the flash of his flawless teeth, the tones of his deep magnetic voice, had imparted a flavour in the highest degree romantic to the illness ; a meaning to the hand-mirror, a fillip to the toilet even when the thermometer registered 103. That voice which had enquired so professionally, so embarrassingly : What about the bowels ? now pressed for a dance—two dances. Numbers 11 and 17 were booked. And hard on his heels arrived Jim Thomson, son of a neighbouring squire, home on leave from his regiment in India, his profile un-intellectual, his conversation lacking in interest, but his long loose limbs most apt and graceful in the dance. Numbers 8 and 9 were booked.

Well, that was better. A bit easier now to
look about at other people. What with the
ones Reggie would in decency be bound to ask
for, one would be spared utter humiliation.
Only . . . when shall I start enjoying myself?
Was there to be nobody, nobody to look forward to ? Dr. Parkes the one bright spot ;
and somehow even he, in spite of all his
charms, wouldn't quite do—not in a human
way. That batch of brother officers—surely
one at least of them would like to be introduced. There were three of them lolling in
a group against the mantelpiece, laughing
together, doing absolutely nothing about the
dance ; yet several unattached females were
forlornly strewn around the walls. . . . And
I'm the prettiest. . . . How rude they were.
If only Lady Spencer would appear from her
inner chamber. . . . And where, where were
the Heriots ? Oh God ! They were going to
wander in late as usual, after one's programme
had got blocked with bores, stroll up after a
long time with a perfunctory formula of re-
quest, gaily grimace and cheerfully be sorry,
and, duty done, dash back to their own party
for the rest of the evening. Must it be so ?

Would one never hear Tony say, as he said in one's daydreams : Oh, rot ! You've *got* to dance with me ! and seizing one's programme cross out all the trivial names and inscribe his own in their place ?

She watched Olivia and Reggie lifelessly progressing round and round the room. Olivia was rather red in the face, with a sort of congested look, as if she might be struggling with feelings. Was it unhappiness, or the effort to make Reggie keep time ? He held her by a loose handful of dress in the small of the back. The stuff would be damp and crumpled when he let her go. Kate found it in her to spare a moment's pity for her sister. A shame she shouldn't enjoy her first dance. If only Reggie would give her the merest fraction of encouragement, she'd be all right : ready to let bygones be bygones and look on the bright side. For oneself, of course, it was different. . . .

There were the Martins ; and Mary Cooper with her brother . . . all taking the floor : Martins in identical dresses of arsenic green satin. What a mistake. A mistake too, really, to leave off their spectacles and look so very blind. All the neighbours looked somehow rather separated and subdued, as if conscious of being local goats divided from house-party sheep ; or the stones in a pot of plum jam, put in to fill up. But surely, once Lady Spencer came she would put everything right. A good plan, perhaps, to go back and sit in the other room so as to jog her memory. Keeping close to the wall, she made her way back to the door, and found her way blocked by a group of people coming out.

Tony Heriot and his twin brothers David and Bill, and some girls.

Tony was just beside her, but he didn't notice her. He was buttoning his gloves and bending, with his usual broad grin, to talk to a very short girl in black. The girl had a great deal of coppery hair, elaborately waved and dressed, overweighting her slight figure. Surely that hair belonged to . . . Yes, it was. It was Etty.

Too startled and confused to speak, Kate stood still, staring at her cousin. At last Etty's eyes fell on her, first blank, then struggling with some suppressed mixture of feelings towards joyful recognition.

' *Darling !* '

167

'Etty! Where did you come from? I didn't know—why didn't you let me know?'

'My sweet, *nobody's* more staggered than myself.' Clasping Kate's hands, she drew her aside. 'I'll explain, angel. Of course if I'd realized I'd have written *at once*. But it was like this. I just happened to meet Tony at a night club last week, and he said *wouldn't* I come down for their little shoot and a dance, and, my dear, it *absolutely* went out of my head *where* he lived and *who* his people were—you know my vagueness, darling—and as Podge was going down too, I simply *hopped* into his car yesterday and set off, and *next* thing I knew we were driving through a town and I said to Podge *where's* this and he said Tulverton— and then, my dear, of course I realized. I said to Tony directly I arrived : My dear, I *suppose* you realize I've got the divinest pair of cousins—especially *one*—' she squeezed Kate's hand—' *not* more than five miles away. And he actually said he hardly knew you. So I said : *this* must be remedied. I was going to ring up *first* thing to-morrow if I didn't see you to-night. You know, I simply *hardly* can realize you're out. It makes me feel most *passée.* And has darling Aunt Ethel really begun to countenance these dissipations, darling ? *What* good news ! Are you starting a *round* of frivolity ? '

' Not much chance.'

Kate tried not to suspect dear Etty of some disingenuousness. It was fairly obvious she had not expected her country-mouse cousins to appear at such a grand party. Still, one must be thankful for present good. She went on :

' Fancy your staying with the Heriots. You never told me you knew them.'

' My lamb, I *didn't* till a few months ago. We stayed in the same house-party for New-market—and then of course you know how it is in London—one always *bumps* into people again. He's *rather* lamb-like, isn't he ? Of course, *much* too youthful for me. I tell him I consider myself his *governess.* The *very* thing for you, darling—neighbours too—it's simply *indicated.* Now I *count* on you to take him off my hands, or my poor old Podge will be *gnashing.* It's too idiotic to be so green-eyed, particularly over a *suckling* like Tony and those lamb-like *embryos* of twins—but I suppose he can't help it.'

' Who is Podge ? '

' Oh, darling, surely I've told you about Podge ? '

' No, never. Is he new ? '

' Mercy, no. Antediluvian. But he clings rather. That's him over there with rather a *pudding* face. He's quite sweet, really. But not exciting.'

' Is he awfully in love with you ? '

Kate scrutinized a solemn young man planted in the doorway. He had a heavy chin and a large slow-motion grey eye. For the first time one of Etty's loves was there before one in the flesh. Rather disappointing, really—not nearly so exciting as those Etty frequently described. He looked vacant, and rather threateningly obstinate, like somebody saying : I'm waiting.

' Well, yes—*definitely* attached. I tell him at least once a month : Not if you were my *last* hope this side the tomb—but it doesn't make any difference. He's the kind who think they've only got to go on turning up and they'll *wear* you down in the end. Still, he's quite sweet and useful. Darling, *what* joy to talk to you again. I tell you what—we'll sit

out a dance together later on and have a
thorough gossip. You look *too* divine, of course—
You make me jealous. I suppose Olivia isn't
here ? '

' Yes, she is. She's dancing. We brought a
partner.'

' A partner ? *Darling,* what bursting and
blossoming ! Now *who* is he ? Is he attractive ? '

' Oh *no !* He's Mother's godson. We'd
never seen him before. He's going to be a
curate.'

Etty gave vent to the anticipated shriek.

' Oh, but how *divine !* You *must* introduce
me. Do you *think* he'd say a prayer with me
if I asked him ? My very first love was a
vicar who prepared me for confirmation at
school. I *adored* him. How *difficult* for you,
though. Never mind.' She looked over her
shoulder and beckoned to Tony with a lift of
the eyebrows and a roguish smile. ' Here's
Tony coming to *tear* us apart. Tony ! ' Her
sparkling, light hazel eyes, rayed round with
starry black lashes, teased and challenged him.
' We were just talking about you.'

' Were you ? ' He smiled with an awkward

good-humoured ease characteristic of him.
'Well, I think it's about time you stopped.'

'Now *this* is my cousin Kate Curtis,' said
Etty triumphantly, ' if you haven't met before.'

'How do you do? As a matter of fact, I
believe we have met, haven't we?' His smile
was broad and diffident.

' I believe we have,' said Kate.

Etty shot her an encouraging nod, rolled her
eyes, slipped away. They saw her flit up to
Podge and lay a coaxing hand upon his lapel.
Next moment she had nestled into his arm
and they were dancing.

There was a silence. Tony said :

' Haven't seen you for ages.'

' No, I know.'

' Been away? '

' Oh no. We never go away. You—haven't
been here much, I suppose, have you? '

' Oh, off and on. Not an awful lot. Came
down for the partridges in October.'

' Oh yes. We sometimes—we hear the guns.'
She hesitated ; then added very shyly : ' We
can see you, too, from our garden, when
you're in the big turnip-field.'

' Oh, really? ' After an effort he remembered where she lived. 'Yes, I suppose you would.'

Suddenly he looked as if something had tickled his fancy. Then he said, his eyes dancing :

'Why didn't you wave to me ? '

He said it in such a funny, quick, teasing way—it sounded so nice. She felt a smile spread all over her. But she couldn't think of a thing to say. In the end she said, looking up at him :

'You never looked.'

'Well, I will next time, so mind you do.'

'All right.'

They beamed at one another.

'As a matter of fact,' she said, 'I shan't be at home much longer. I'm going to Paris.'

'Oh, are you ? What are you going to do there ? '

'Learn French, I suppose.'

'Not you ! You'll just have a high old time. I've heard all about these finishing schools— isn't that what they call them ? Fat lot of school there is about them.'

'Oh, I shall have to work,' she said.

But he simply grinned at her. No point in telling him one was only going to a professor's family. It sounded so stuffy. It might put him off.

' Any dances left ? ' he said.

' I think so.' She held her programme up so that he couldn't see. He waited, his pencil hovering. ' As a matter of fact,' she said, ' I'm not dancing this one.'

' Good. Nor am I. I must just see—' he looked round—' oh, it's all right. Twins doing their duty.'

The twins had taken the floor with a bobbed-haired girl apiece, and were performing vigorous and complicated steps. Obviously they'd been having lessons. They spun, tottered, stopped dead, side-slipped, swooped diagonally, neatly controlling large feet and overgrown limbs, their hair sleeked with oil, their cheerful twin faces gaping mildly, blank with concentration.

' Well, shall we ? ' he said.

They started to dance.

' I say, look at them.' Amused, he watched his brothers. ' It's their latest craze. They keep a gramophone in their bedrooms and one in the bathroom, and start in as soon as they get up.' He added with pride, 'Aren't they nimble, though ? '

' They must practise a lot with the same partners.'

A special gramophone for the bathroom. . . . What a delirious standard.

' I suppose they do. I don't know. I don't see much of them these days. . . . They've been at it all day with those girls. None of them ever says a word. Dancing dulls the brain a bit, I think, don't you ? '

Not his girls, then. He sounded beautifully bored with them.

' I suppose it's just a phase,' she said.

' Oh yes. We all go through them, don't we ? As a matter of fact, I've been having an anti-dance phase this last year.'

' Have you ? Have you still got it ? ' She looked up at him. Her eyes, he thought, were like green water, lucid, refreshing.

' Well, I believe it's passing off. Seems to be to-night at least.' He gave a little laugh. ' But, you know—you get fed up.'

' Yes, I know. When you've done a thing a lot. . . .'

'Besides—well, I don't know. I suppose you get older.'

'Yes, that's it.'

'Anyway,' she said after a bit, 'you don't seem out of practice.'

'Don't I? Thank you for those kind words. 'Fraid I can't compete with the very latest, though. But you're so frightfully easy to dance with.'

He tightened his arm slightly and swung her round a corner.

'Am I? I'm glad.'

'Going to the hunt ball?'

'No, I'm not.'

'Going to be away?'

'Oh no. Just not going.'

'What a pity!'

They danced in silence again.

He said :

'I'd no idea Etty was your cousin.'

'Oh yes. My first cousin.' Obviously this had enhanced prestige. She added languidly : 'She's my greatest friend, really.'

'Is she? She's most awfully nice. Such fun.'

'Oh yes, Etty's sweet.'

'She looks so tiny and frail, but she's game for anything.'

176

' I know.' She wished suddenly for a more delicate frame. After a bit, unable to resist, she added : ' Of course she's not really frail in the least, you know. She's as strong as a horse.'

' I suppose she is,' he agreed in an unconcerned way : so unconcerned that she regretted the flavour of betrayal.

' Do you still hunt ? '

' Hunt ? Rather. At least, whenever I can. Of course, now I'm in London I don't get much chance. Only every other Saturday.'

' How sickening. What do you do in London ? '

' Oh, work away, you know. Nine-thirty till six in the City every blinking day. Slavery, isn't it ? '

' Yes, it *is*.'

' What a corking band ! '

He tightened his arm again to swing her round a corner.

§ 3

The band stopped playing. To Olivia's relief, nobody clapped this time for an encore. The floor was emptying, and Reggie stood beside her, hands in pockets, not suggesting any move. She felt hot already, flushed and flustered. Her heart made a heavy thumping all over her. They hadn't been at all a graceful couple. Each time a hitch occurred, she'd said : Sorry. He never replied : My fault, so that she felt more and more convicted of clumsy incompetence. The mark of a good dancer is her ability to adapt herself to any partner. This had been mere struggle and discomfort. She thought with terror : I don't believe I know how to do it.

'Fine room this.' He threw a connoisseur's eye around. 'Handsome proportions.'

'Yes, isn't it lovely?'

She saw themselves reflected in one of the huge wall-mirrors ; and either it's distorting or I'm looking extremely thick, squat and red all over.

'I believe I'd like a drink of lemonade,' she said. 'I feel awfully thirsty.'

'Sound idea.'

He said this quite jovially, and she took heart again, leading the way to the dining-room. There was nobody there except a number of silent black waiters motionless behind the buffet. They all looked rather surprised, and the one who poured out the lemonade seemed to do so grudgingly as if he were saying : Rather premature, surely ?

'Any cup?' asked Reggie, questing like a prawn over the groaning board, seizing here a foie-gras roll, there a chocolate éclair.

'Yes, sir.'

The waiter was shocked. He filled a glass from a glorious jug of golden fruit-sprinkled liquid and handed it with a cold expression.

'Thanks. . . . Animals not started feeding yet.'

The waiter said nothing. Perhaps he didn't hear ; perhaps he wished to discourage vulgar familiarity. When one thought of dear Lady Spencer and the other dowagers it did sound rather misplaced. . . .

Irresistibly she was drawn to a plate of *petits fours*. After looking at them for some time, she surreptitiously took one. It was delicious. She took another ; then gulped the rest of her lemonade. But it could not cool her burning cheeks.

'Try one of these,' said Reggie, with his mouth full. 'They're jolly good.'

' No, thanks.'

She began to long to lean against something cold. A nude female figure in marble
by the door looked the very thing. She
went and laid her cheek against one thigh.
Reggie remained by the table. He must be
rather greedy. . . . Oh, the hours and hours
ahead ! . . . Instantly, at the thought, she felt
herself turning and tossing on a dark feverish
sea, all bearings lost : a worse disintegration
even than she had envisaged. Keep calm.
Carry it off. Here against the statue, just at
the cold spot of contact, she felt a core begin
to reassemble. I am still here. Her beating
heart quietened down.

Gusts of giggles came suddenly through the
door. She turned and saw the Martins, Phyl
and Dolly, and with them a young man with
flaming red hair, in naval uniform. It must
be the one they called their middy cousin.
Good old Martins. When all else was lost,
their presence could always be counted on at
the buffet.

' First in as usual ! ' cried Phyl. ' Oh no,
we've actually been beaten. Oh, it's Olivia.
Hullo, hullo, hullo ! What are *you* up to ? '

They bore down upon her in their massive bright green upholstery, stared at her, went off into peals of laughter.

'What have you done? . . . your face . . .'

'What? What?'

She felt positively faint. It must be the powder, coagulated in the heat or something. No wonder I'm not getting on well. Reggie must have been ashamed to be seen dancing with me.

'Covered . . . an *enormous* black smudge . . . all down your face . . . what have you been . . .' They were helpless.

'Here,' said the young man, very quiet and polite but twinkling, offering a clean white handkerchief. 'It'll soon come off.'

'Look.' Dolly wiped her eyes and held up the pocket mirror out of her bag. 'Something's come off on you.'

Olivia looked. A wild streak of dust splashed her right cheek.

'*Oh!* Good *gracious!*' She rubbed desperately. It came off. 'It's that statue.' She indicated the round-limbed naked but modest figure on the pedestal. 'I've been—I was leaning against it.'

' *Leaning* against it ? What on earth for ? The girl's loopy.' They were off again, louder than ever.

' To get cool.'

The face of the red-haired young man seemed to be going to burst with twinkles ; but he didn't laugh. He only looked up at the statue with a very queer expression, and said softly :

' Good idea.'

' You always were eccentric, my poor child,' sighed Dolly, fanning herself with her programme. ' I fear for you. . . . All the same,' she went on, nudging her sister, ' it daon't saiy much for 'er Lidyship's 'ousemaids, do it ? '

' Nao. You'd reelly think they'd give the *limbs* a rub over when company's expected. I can understand them not caring to put a duster to the—er—ahem !—the *trunk*.'

' Where I was once I got acquainted with the third laidy's-maid to a duchess. Believe it or believe it not, they kept a special staff there to polish up the statchery—footmen for the mailes, 'ousemaids for the femailes.'

They giggled all together. Blessed Martins, comfortably asserting themselves in these foreign surroundings, regardless of disapproving waiters ; making their own circle of sound, hilarious, coarse-fibred normality wherever they went. Everything began to seem itself again.

'This here is cousin Maurice,' said Phyl, slapping the young man on the bottom. 'Commonly called Tomato, because he looks so Spanish. For the love of Mike, take him off our hands for a bit.'

'May I have a dance ? ' said Maurice, polite and attentive.

At once she knew he liked her. She didn't feel a bit shy or anxious.

'I'd love to. What about the next one ? '

'Splendid. Thanks awfully.'

'I believe it's starting now.'

'Oh, come on. My favourite waltz. Are you keen on waltzes ? '

'I love them. I like them much better than fox-trots.'

'Pity your reds clash so,' said Dolly. 'However, don't let it worry you. . . . Oh, sorry ! ' Stepping back, she had trodden heavily on the foot of Reggie, who had joined them unobserved.

'Oh ! ' Olivia had forgotten all about him. 'Can I introduce— This is Mr. Kershaw.'

The Martins were simply delighted to see
him. They seemed to surround, fall in upon,
overwhelm him in their eagerness to cement
the bonds of friendship. He'd be all right
with them. They'd probably say afterwards
how awfully jolly he was ; or if not, shout
with laughter in his face, call him a perfect
scream.

'Well, me for an ice !' shouted Phyl.

'I can recommend them,' said Reggie, quite
eagerly and boyishly.

He returned with them to the table, looking
as he walked between them like a small black
beetle wandering among a flourishing bed of
melons.

They'd be there for some time. They
wouldn't care what the waiters thought.

'Is my face quite clean now ? ' She lifted
it for his inspection.

'Rather. Top hole.'

'What a lucky thing you saw me in time !
I'm sorry I dirtied your clean hanky.'

She could laugh now.

They hurried back to the ballroom.

He was a very rapid dancer. He danced on
his toes and hopped like a grasshopper. This,

combined with his hair and his freckles, made
him comically conspicuous. He was not a
romantic figure : in fact, for some reason, he
made one think of some domestic fowl—a hen
or a turkey. But he was very nice indeed.
His beautiful manners and responsive open
face were restful and encouraging. Once one
had managed to catch his pace one found it
easier to dance quick than slow. It was quite
exhilarating, whisking and springing round
the room.

They had two dances together. During
the second, she caught Kate's eye for the
first time since their separation, and was
able to give her a cheerful wink. Kate
was dancing with Tony Heriot—none other :
so that was all right. She looked quite
rapt and shining, and almost forgot to wink
back.

After the second dance, they sat out on the
stairs.

He said :

' Been to any shows in London lately ? '

' No, I haven't just lately,' she said brightly.
' Have you ? '

' I saw *For Love or Money* last week. Topping

show. Fay Monkton's simply ripping in it.
You ought to see it.'

' I must try to.' But now she felt bound to
admit : ' As a matter of fact, I don't often
go to London. Practically never.'

After a bit he said :

' Ever run over to Brooklands from here ? '

' No,' she said carefully, concealing a blank.
' No, I never do.'

' Too late this year, of course. You ought to
go next spring when there's a big day on. That
is, if you're interested in that sort of thing.'

' Oh yes, I am. I must go.'

A big day at Brooklands ? . . . After a bit
she said :

' Are you going to many dances this
Christmas ? '

' I expect I shall get in a few. Are you ? '

' Not very many, I don't think.'

' Ever been to a dance in a battleship ? '

' Oh no, never.'

' We gave a dance last year during Navy
week. It was a rattling good show.' He
added mildly : ' You ought to come down for
it next time.'

' Oh, it would be lovely ! '

She glowed, thinking : this was the way of
life : when you made no effort for a success,
it dropped into your hands.

'Get Dolly or Phyl to buzz you down.'

He left it at that. It sounded rather vague,
really—not very likely to come to anything.

One ought to ask him questions about the
Navy. But after asking what ship he was on,
and he had said gently, Not 'on'—'in,' and
how long leave he had, and if he was ever sea-
sick, and if he had been to China, there seemed
nothing more to say without exposing an abyss
of ignorance. So she remained silent, and so
did he. But it was quite a nice silence. He
wasn't an exacting person. His simple light-
blue eye looked outward, uncritically ranging
over his surroundings. He didn't want to be
absorbed in her alone. This was a little
disappointing.

The stairs were crowded with couples, and
down in the hall below Rollo and another
young man were sparring together.

She said :

'That's Rollo Spencer.'

'Is it ? ' he said mildly. 'His sister's a jolly
pretty girl, isn't she ? '

' Yes, Marigold's very pretty.'

' Could you point her out ? '

' I'm afraid I can't see her anywhere at the moment.'

' Never mind. There's a lot of jolly pretty girls here to-night.'

' Yes, there are.'

' Can you introduce me to that one in pink ? ' He indicated a fluffy baby-faced creature sitting on the landing.

She said apologetically :

' I'm afraid I don't know her.'

' Never mind.'

The music had begun again. Extraordinary how it invaded every part of this big house. There was no escape from it. Take your partners, it blared. Leave your last one, take your next one. . . . My programme is a blank.

They got up to make way for the down-trooping swarm. He's off. He's not going to ask me for another. . . . She felt her smile twist and freeze. But suddenly he said :

' Could you spare me one in the second half ? '

' Oh yes, I'd love to, thanks.'

188

He booked number 15, thanked her and left her, threading his way lightly through the crowd, jaunty, modest, self-assured, intent on the evening's job.

§ 4

Alone once more.

She went and sat against the wall. Lady Spencer sailed out of the little room, brushing Olivia in the flow and sweep of her passage.

'Oh, Olivia dear. . . .' She paused, reflective, a hand on Olivia's shoulder. 'I want to introduce such an interesting . . . Come with me, dear.' She took her arm lightly and led her back into the little room. 'The son of some new neighbours of ours. . . . Such a charming . . . very clever. A *poet*. He doesn't seem to know many . . . so do be kind to him.'

They approached a youth standing upon the hearthrug, posed in a sombre and defensive attitude. The first thing one noticed was his hair. He wore it over his forehead in a crooked fringe.

Lady Spencer said, with her most compelling graciousness :

' Olivia dear, this is Mr. Jenkin—Peter Jenkin, whom I was just telling you about. Mr. Jenkin, Miss Olivia Curtis.'

He bowed from his waist, in silence. He looked resentful, not to say definitely hostile.

' I'm sure you two will find a great deal to talk about.'

Off she sailed again, so powerful and so certain, leaving in her wake a vacuum. There didn't seem anything at all to say to Mr. Jenkin. She fumbled with her programme.

He said :

' I don't dance.'

After a moment's collapse, she felt emboldened to say :

' Then why did you come ? ' She didn't say it boldly, and she blushed.

He shrugged his shoulders.

' Oh—the houses of the great, you know. We can't resist a peep at high life, can we ? I've never achieved it before.'

How sarcastic he sounded. . . . He didn't move his lips in speaking, and his voice came out of the roof of his mouth in a hollow, clipped, extinguished way, difficult to catch.

' Yes, it's my first dance too.'

He shot a glance at her for the first time— suspicious. He had queer eyes, greenish-brown and fiery, deep-set, with a slight cast. He closed them, blinking rapidly for a second, and simultaneously jerking his head. He said :

' To be quite honest, I suppose it was the usual emotional bludgeoning. Do go for my sake. Why do you never want to please me— and all that. She knows I can't stand up against it.'

' Who ? '

' My mother,' he said sulkily, as if suppressing an impatient ' of course.' He blinked and jerked again. ' She's the most outrageous woman in the world. I do everything she tells me.'

Good gracious. . . .

He went on broodingly :

' The temptation is to give up struggling. Simply accept the fact that she's ruined one's life. . . .'

' Are you—haven't you got a father ? '

' My father I merely dislike.' Blink, jerk.

'Or rather despise. But I'm sorry for him—my God, I am!—bloody sorry.' He nodded sombrely. 'She's cooked his goose all right.'

What a revelation. . . . What a shock. . . . Life at first hand. Telling a perfect stranger, too. No wonder he looked so queer. Trouble had unhinged him. That nervous trick with his eyes . . . and using such bad language. . . . One must show quiet sympathy, not appear shocked or surprised.

'How rotten for you. It must be simply terrible to have such—not to get on with one's parents.'

'Oh, it's just the dear old Œdipus again. We can't get away from it, can we? I suppose one might be analysed.' He shrugged his shoulders.

He was talking absolute gibberish now. Perhaps he really was a little mad.

'Of course she's had a very unsatisfactory sex-life—for a woman of her temperament. It's made her definitely hysterical. And I'm the only son. So, naturally . . .' Blink, jerk. 'Of course I'm possessive too—violently so. I take after her. She's a brilliant creature—beautiful—the most divine companion. I get my creative gifts from her. We have Russian blood.' He passed a languid delicate hand through his fringe.

It must be the Russian blood that made his complexion so sallow and his skull so shallow and flat. His lips were wide and flat, his cheekbones high ; and he was a queer shape— heavy about the shoulders, with long arms and short legs.

' I've got foreign blood too,' she said ; ' one of my great-grandmothers was French.'

He took no notice of this.

She tried timidly :

' You write, don't you ? '

' Yes.' He sounded offended again.

' How thrilling.' Better not mention one's own paltry efforts. ' Poetry or prose ? '

' Both. My poems are better known.'

She said with enthusiasm :

' I *should* love to read them.'

He looked at her, still gloomily but with a glimmer of relenting.

' Perhaps you haven't heard of *Attack*.'

' No, I'm afraid I——'

' The review we started last term—Brian Carruthers and myself.' Blink, jerk. ' Car-

ruthers is editor—I'm sub-editor. Wilkes is in
it too—Wilkes of the O.U.D.S., you know—the
designer.' (Wilkes of the what? It sounded
like owds. . . .) 'Our aim is of course to
create an entirely modern aesthetics—assert the
new forms.' Blink, jerk of particular violence.
' We break altogether with tradition. Of course
Cambridge has nothing comparable. . . .'

He said all this in a very haughty and sulky
way, almost as if he couldn't be bothered to
talk about it. But he went on all the same :
' I sent a copy of the first number to Beckett
Adye—the critic—you know. He thought it
reached a very high level. He liked my poems
particularly.'

He glanced again at her attentive face and
added, more kindly :

' If you're interested, I'll send you a copy.
Let me have your address.'

' Oh, thanks most frightfully. I should
simply love that.'

How very exciting. . . . New worlds opening.
He must be simply terrifically clever. And I
haven't disgraced myself at all. He must quite
like me, to think me worthy of a copy.

' Read Carruthers first, then me. I supplement him aesthetically—*and* psychologically. Possibly you know his work.'

' I'm afraid I don't.'

' He published three poems in a limited edition last year. Difficult stuff, but, my God, it's great ! It fluttered the dovecotes, I can tell you.' A sardonic smile twisted his lips. ' But his latest work goes deeper. It's definitely more significant. A little obscure perhaps if you're not familiar with his extremely subtle suggestive method . . . approximating in fact to *unconscious* direction. . . .' He considered this statement critically, and gave it his sanction with a nod ; adding in quite a confiding way : ' My God, he brings it off, though! I'll send you a copy. Don't try to understand him. Let his pattern sink in. Actually it's his autobiography. But it's still unfinished.'

' When will it be finished ? '

' Ah, there's the rub. Sometimes he's uncreative for months together. He's definitely neurotic. He ought to be analysed.'

' He must be very interesting.'

' The point about Carruthers is that he derives from no one. His meaning and purpose are entirely his own. Now, I myself confess to various influences. There's definitely a trace of Blakeney in my early work—I can see it. But I've definitely thrown it off. My last two poems are very good. I'll send them to you. What's your name ? Berenice ? '

' No, it isn't. Why should you think so ? '

' Why not ? I dare say actually it's Ivy or Joyce or Betty. I prefer not to hear. I choose my own names for my friends.'

' What do you call Carruthers ? ' (He's classing me with his friends. . . . Ought I to have said *Mr.* Carruthers ? . . .)

' Dimitri.' Blink, jerk, offended voice. ' He's pure Dostoievsky, of course.'

What could that mean ? . . . Something very flattering and unusual. It was awfully nice of him to admire Carruthers and his poetry so much. He must be very unselfish. Of course Berenice was an uncommon name too. Was it meant in a complimentary way ? One must just hope.

He took a yellow cigarette from a black enamel case, and lit it. He seemed brighter altogether, and hadn't blinked for several minutes. He looked through the open door towards the ballroom, and his lip curled.

'What a spectacle!' He snorted. 'Makes one sick.'

Whatever could be wrong? She dared not ask. She remained silent and looked too, seeing a lot of people dancing a fox-trot in a restrained but cheerful way : whereas he saw a sight that turned his stomach.

'The unreality of it!' He gave an unexpected shrill cackle. 'My God, though, it has its humorous side. What's-her-name now— that bosomy tin-plated dowager, yearning over us with her bowels of condescension. . . .' He paused, pleased with this. 'All these well-diluted debs—guaranteed wholesome and sedative. They're enough to make a cat laugh.' He cackled again. 'And what a remarkable collection of animal fragments! . . . tusks, paws, heads, tails, horns, skulls and what not. I've been admiring them. And the pictures — horsy ancestors, ancestral horses — such an interesting study. And these young serving-men in fancy dress — they *enthral* me.'

She acknowledged his wit with a smile ; but she was unnerved. Such a totally fresh point of view, so disquieting and subversive. *Tin-*

plated dowager. . . . . Could he really mean . . . ?
He could.   He looked quite genial now.

'That's my sister, the one in green with a
little cape.'   Surely his sarcastic generaliza-
tions would not apply to Kate.   She was
dancing with Dr. Parkes.   He studied her with
a sharp cold eye.

'Um.   Chaste-looking girl.   Quite a nymph.
Barley-water nymph.   God !   There's just
enough sex appeal in this room to tickle up
a canary.   What's the matter with you English
virgins ? '   He turned and stared at her.
'How old are you ? '

'Seventeen.'

He puffed at his cigarette, blowing the smoke
out through his wide satyr's nostrils and looking
her up and down.

'You've got possibilities.   But you don't give
yourself a chance.   Why don't you make up ?
If there's one thing in the world I find dis-
tressing it's these schoolgirl complexions.   You
ought to take a lesson from my friend Inez.
God, she's got style !   I choose her clothes for
her.   You ought to meet her.'

She was silent, thinking how much she would
prefer not to meet Inez.

'That dress of yours, now,' he said. 'It won't do, will it? Honestly . . .?'

She attempted a smile; but she felt strangled.

'I'm afraid it doesn't fit very well.'

He went on:

'Besides, the colour. So *crude*. I never let Inez wear anything but black at night. Occasionally white.'

'I don't like black,' she said in a weak, high, defiant voice. He disregarded this and continued unmoved:

'I dare say it's not your fault. You've never been taught. It takes a man to teach a woman how to dress. The majority of them don't develop a clothes-sense till they've had a lover. Or a face either, for that matter. No woman under twenty-five's worth looking at.'

He wasn't studying her any more—that was the only comfort. Oh, to rip off this scorching dress, to sink through the carpet! Of course it was absurd to take him seriously. What could a man like him know about clothes? Kate would have known how to put him in his place in two two's. But I don't feel like that. I can't feel indignant at his awful rudeness. . . . His cold and somehow acid voice was like a probe searching into sore places : but she must bare her breast. She was his appointed and—yes—in the last recoil his willing victim. She had to hear, had to suffer him, because he was so certain. And I'm never certain. This was the truth about the dress, then—about the whole business : I'm ludicrous, a sort of bungling amateur. I can't compete with the real thing.

It can't be helped. Good for my conceit. I must just . . . I've got my own things : home ; and my hyacinths that'll bloom by Christmas ; books ; and Monsieur Berton saying, My favourite pupil ; and writing poetry. . . .

She began to bleed secretly in her self-esteem. She felt it : a lesion through which virtue was going to seep away unstanched. But it must be disregarded. She felt quite composed again, unusually so, in a surface way.

The band had stopped, and a number of couples invaded the room and disposed themselves in chairs and sofas. He looked round upon them under lowered brows, then moved to the door, saying loudly :

'I suppose one can get a drink in this house.'

She noticed that he walked with a limp, as if one leg were shorter than the other. Poor boy, no wonder he didn't dance. He was probably embittered, like Byron. One must excuse everything.

In the almost deserted ballroom, several young men, the sort who looked like Rollo's brother officers, were galloping about kicking their legs up and uttering hunting-cries. 'Nothing like an Englishman for a rag, is there?' He jerked his shoulders in an elaborate display of ironic laughter. 'Damn good sportsmen! With any luck they'll break up some chairs and things soon. Just for the joke of it.'

Perhaps it was rather disgusting: so noisy and silly. All the same, but for him it might have seemed rather funny. In fact his comments had startled away the smile with which she had all too leniently greeted their antics. How incessantly on one's guard one had to be with clever people; what bad taste one could show without knowing it.

He went limping over the floor, contemptuously skirting a couple now doing a kind of step dance in the middle of the room. Just as they reached the opposite doorway, Lady Spencer appeared within it, summoned by the noise, prepared for action, her presence particularly imposing, her eye veiled with purpose.

' Aunt Sibyl ! ' one of the dancers sprang towards her, arms outstretched. ' The very person I was longing for.'

' Archie, what's all this noise ? '

Her voice was severe, but her face relaxed. She looked at him indulgently ; then, seeing Olivia, detained her with a friendly hand upon her shoulder. Mr. Jenkin passed on through the door without one backward look.

' It's all right, Aunt Sibyl, I swear. Don't look so like a distressed gentlewoman. It's just the exuberance of youth. You intoxicate me in your silver gown—that's what it is. Who can hold a candle to you ?—no one. Now, angel, come with me and show this blighter how to dance a reel. Come on now. Rouse up your Scots blood.'

' You ridiculous boy.' Smiling, frowning, half yielding, half protesting, she let him lead her forward. ' The idea ! '

' Ah, do ! To please me.'

He confronted her, his face brimming with laughter, coaxing, radiating some quality that drew one's eye, one's smile, one's will. ' One—two—three ! '

And actually — actually there was Lady Spencer, hands on hips, breaking into the jaunty steps of a brisk reel, footing it opposite him most lightly and skilfully, with perfect dignity, her eyes laughing back at him.

' No more ! No more ! ' She stopped, panting a little, shaking her head as they all clapped. ' Archie, you are a *terrible* boy. How could you make me so forget myself ? I haven't danced for years.'

' Then it's time you started again.'

' Ah dear !—I could once. I used to love it.'

' So you do still, of course. You're superb. We'll dance together for the rest of the evening.'

She said with sudden firmness :

' Now, be quiet. No more nonsense. You're not doing your duty at all nicely, and I'm not pleased with you.'

' Oh, darling ! ' He clasped his hands,

gazing at her with mock penitence. 'Aren't I pulling my weight?'

'Now, I didn't invite you to spend the evening romping by yourself. You ought to know better. You're behaving like a school-boy. Why don't you dance with some of these charming girls?'

'Oh, I will, I will! Forgive! They are so charming, I must dance with them all.'

'And George too. You ought to be ashamed of yourselves.'

'I'm sorry, Lady Spencer.'

George sounded sheepish. He was a fairish, tallish, average looking young man with a toothbrush moustache.

'Come both of you and be introduced to a great friend of ours, Olivia Curtis.'

'How are you? How are you? Delighted.'

Archie gave her an elaborate bow, his eyes vague and sparkling, looking desperately amused, and yet somehow as if he weren't quite attending. He said pressingly:

'Nineteen. Number Nineteen. My lucky number.' He laughed.

'Yes, I'd love to.'

She beamed. For of course, though he had

changed a lot, she had recognized him at
once : Archie of the broom. Naturally he's
forgotten me. I won't remind him till we
dance together.

'Thank you so much—*so* much.'

But he didn't write it down. He didn't
seem to have a programme. He smoothed his
hair and fanned himself with his handkerchief,
looking at Lady Spencer with a funny teasing
challenging expression.

'May I have the next one?' said George
with formality.

'Yes, I'd love to.'

It seemed almost a miracle. The hand-
somest man in the room, the very person one
would have picked first anywhere, any day,
yet never hoped to acquire. . . . And George
as well—nothing like so thrilling, but still, so
well-groomed and superior. . . . Kate'll be
quite jealous. In deep and grateful affection
she looked up to smile at Lady Spencer.
Bosomy tin-plated . . . how could he ! Out
of the corner of an eye she could see him in
the passage, standing stiffly against the wall,
looking bilious and solitary. I don't care. I
shan't bother about him. He's horrid.

Lady Spencer said, very quietly, as if she didn't want to be overheard :

' Archie, you will be good, won't you ? '
She searched his face, looking serious. He answered loudly :

' Yes, Aunt Sibyl, I will.'

He sounded a tiny bit sheepish and impatient, and he turned away from her.

' Are you all right, dear ? ' She patted Olivia. ' Enjoying yourself ? '

' Oh yes, thank you.'

Supposing that one could conceivably wish to be malicious, one might perhaps feel that dear Lady Spencer was making a statement rather than asking a question, scarcely listening for the inevitable enthusiastic affirmative of any guest at any party of hers. But how could one wish to be so ? She was so gracious ; every action she performed was so fitting and so right ; she could suddenly step down from her throne and startle one with a step dance and look young and laughing, almost mischievous and flirtatious, yet be only the more superbly herself—one must adore her.

' Did you and Mr. Jenkin——? '

Looking round for him with vague benevolence, her eye was arrested by the sight of his hunched crooked sulky-looking back view flinging down the passage out of sight. (Queer: he wasn't limping any more.) She paused, looking momentarily absent and reflective, then smiled, nodded and sailed away to join another tall grey-haired matron in black, whose appearance bore a family likeness to her own. She took her arm :

'Blanchie, that graceless boy of yours . . .'

They passed out of earshot, moving serenely, unassailably in that place they lived in, that place from which Mr. Jenkin, did he but know it, had just been dropped, without any fuss, for ever—a place where one's sons didn't drink too much or one's guests overstep the bounds of permissible eccentricity by crude anti-social displays of hostility.

Archie flung himself into a chair, shaking with laughter, mopping his face, saying to George :

'Isn't she divine? Isn't she *divine*? I swear I'd rather—' he lowered his voice abruptly, glanced round—'than any girl in the room.' After a moment he added : 'I bet I could too.'

They murmured and laughed together.

Retiring discreetly, Olivia heard him say :

' Tip the others the wink. There's a private supply in my bedroom.'

She found Mary Cooper and her brother in the hall, and sat talking to them till the band struck up again.

§ 5

George was not the kind of partner who cared to talk while dancing. Once one realized that there was no necessity to keep up a flow of small talk, it was quite a pleasure to remain silent and fit oneself to his simple but correct style ; just a gliding walk, with a little halt and flourish at the turns, very easy to manage.

After the dance, sitting beside her on the landing, he politely offered her a cigarette, lit one himself, and opened the conversation.

' Were you out to-day ? '

' Oh yes.'

' Jolly good day, wasn't it ? At least a rotten morning, but the afternoon was first class.'

' Yes, it was nice.' Rather surprising. It

had been so very wet. But perhaps he liked walking in the rain. ' I love to be out in the rain if I'm dressed for it.'

' Um. Going out on Saturday——? '

' I expect so.' Rather mystifying. ' I go out every day, really.'

' What ? Do you honestly ? ' He looked very much impressed, but at the same time rather incredulous. After a bit of thinking he said :

' You don't live round here, then ? '

' Oh yes. At least, only eight miles away.'

He said respectfully :

' You must be awfully keen. I suppose some days you have a jolly good distance to motor ? '

' Oh no. We haven't got a car.'

He looked absolutely staggered.

' But I didn't know there were more than two packs within fifty miles.'

Bombshells. Death and damnation. Hideous light in darkness. Consternation. Humiliation.

' Oh, I thought you meant . . . I misunderstood. I don't—as a matter of fact, I don't really hunt.'

After a moment he said politely :

' Oh, I see. I couldn't make it out.'

He didn't smile, or otherwise reveal his feelings. He fell silent, and looked at his shoes. She ventured timidly :

' I wish I did. It must be such fun.'

False. Denying acute feelings about foxes to curry favour.

He said relentingly :

' Nothing like it. I'd rather have a good day's hunting than a week's shooting, any day.'

' Yes, I quite agree. It looks so lovely too, doesn't it ? The red coats.'

' The what ? '

' The colour, I mean.'

He said very distinctly, looking straight in front of him :

' Oh, the pink coats.'

' Yes, the pink coats.'

She tried to repeat it indifferently, as if correcting what of course had been a mere unaccountable slip of the tongue. She remembered now too late : coats were pink, dogs were hounds.

But he remained aloof, made a few more perfunctory remarks, left her with alacrity as soon as the music began again. He didn't ask for another dance.

Reggie turned up, looking cheerful, saying in a voice of mild regret, unshadowed by suspicion :

' Unfortunately I've had no luck with your sister. Her programme appears to be completely full.'

§ 6

Supper interval. Martins again, calling heartily from their table :

' Come along you two. Room for a little one.'

Quite a cheerful party, with Maurice, Mary Cooper and her brother, and another rather dim willing youth with spots. It was clear that Phyl and Dolly thought Reggie not only a scream, but awfully jolly as well. He engaged with them in Cockney repartee, and did some conjuring tricks with glasses and knives. No doubt, they brought out the best in him. In his light vein he didn't seem so altogether isolated, so out of touch with human beings. He might be going to be quite popular in his parish, especially at the socials. Kate and I treated him all wrong. We ought to have done some ragging. I don't know how to do it.

' I say, Olivia, who's your shady-looking pal ? '

' Who ? '

' Oh, come off it—you know—with the O-cedar mop coiffure.'

' I suppose you mean Peter Jenkin.'

' And who's Petah Jenkin ? '

' He's a poet.'

' I guessed as much. Either that or an escaped convict.'

There was a shout of laughter.

' He's at Oxford. Do you know him, Reggie ? '

' I beg your pardon.' Engaged in re-plenishing his plate, Reggie hadn't heard. ' Oh, Jenkin—I know him by reputation.' He seemed to be noticing an unpleasant smell.

She said rather aggressively :

' He's frightfully clever.'

' He's a me-ar mass of affectation,' pro-nounced Reggie, almost intoning. ' Thor-oughly undesirable.'

' One of these decadents, I suppose.'

'Distinctly unappetizing specimen, I must say.'

'Never can think why these brainy birds have to make themselves look such frights.'

'Suppose they've got to advertise,' said Maurice mildly. 'Otherwise people 'ud think they were just ordinary chaps.'

'Well, give me the common or garden ones who aren't above indulging in a bath and hair-cut when they need it.'

'Every time.'

'Brains aren't everything, by a long chalk. At least not in my humble opinion.'

'Hear, hear!'

The buzz, the chattering idiocy. . . . If sides must be taken, it was not their side one could take. Of course he was awful, a mass of affectation; and then so cruel; and doing his hair in such a dreadful way. He looked as if he took no exercise. He was an outcast, made for hatred and derision. But—what was it then that made one feel that, with just a few more clues provided, one could get to know him, understand his language? I should soon feel at ease with a person like him; receive his confidence. Be sorry for him. Not think him absurd and contemptible at all. There must be something shady in me too, then, something decadent. I'm different from them, though they don't know it. She felt the cleavage, deep, uneasy. I'm not going to do the things they'll do.

'Hot lobster. By Jove, this is a proper do, and no mistake,' said Maurice. 'Tuck in, girls. Do yourselves justice.'

It was a proper do and no mistake. They did themselves more than justice.

Champagne too. They drank it with grimaces, with giggles and chaff and exclamations. Reggie emptied several glasses.

At the big middle table, that face again, turning slowly this way and that on the long neck, the white dress staring vivid against the scarlet of Rollo's coat. Rollo kept on watching the face. Sometimes it smiled faintly, not looking at him or any one. They didn't talk much. When one looked at them, there seemed no one else in the room—only these two.

'Olivia, you slacker, why didn't you turn up at Guides last week?'

Why not say : Because I preferred to spend the afternoon on the schoolroom sofa reading

East Lynne and eating nut-milk chocolate. . . .
Because I loathe the beastly Guides.

' I had such an awful cold.'

' You know you're a bit of a slacker.
Honestly.' Phyl's voice was cheery but re-
proving.

She blushed darkly. Publicly admonished.

§ 7

Now the evening was at the flood, racing
from room to room. Now the fortunate sailed
with it, serene—doubt, fear allayed. Now if
failure threatened, failure was confirmed. From
now on could be but a declension for such as
faltered and fell aside, caught and borne down
by inauspicious currents, stranded upon islands
empty, arid, salt.

Now Kate rode upon the forward crest, in
certain buoyancy and unwavering light.

Tony said, as they danced :

' Look here, why don't you come to the hunt
ball ? '

She admitted gaily, demurely :

' Nobody's asked me. I can't go alone.'

' Well, look here—can't you come ? I mean

—join our party—come and dine with us first. It's the day after to-morrow.'

' Oh!' She took a deep breath. 'Oh, I would love to. I don't know. Mother's very strict.'

She tried to see herself announcing at home, in a perfectly offhand way : Tony Heriot's asked me to a dance.

' I say, is she really ? Would she object to me, do you think ? '

' I don't know. I shouldn't think she could.'

She glanced up at him, shy, smiling. Their eyes met, they looked into each other's eyes.

' Tell you what—we'll get Etty to ring up.'

' Oh, good idea ! Etty can always get round Mother.'

' Etty'd get round anybody.'

' Yes, she would. I'm sitting out the next dance with her. I'll ask her.'

It didn't matter any more what bouquets he threw to Etty. They were only bouquets. They were Etty's due.

§ 8

No partner for this one. No more hope of getting one now. Quick to the cloakroom,

then, that refuge. It was quite good really
not to have had to seek it before now.

Turning, Olivia saw a heavy young man
with a moustache and a bulging slow-motion
grey eye strolling towards her. He stopped in
front of her, and said, speaking through his
nose, scarcely moving his lips, adjusting his tie
and looking over her head :

' Take a turn with me ? '

She said gratefully :

' Oh, thank you, I'd love to.'

What tremendous luck. . . . He must have
—could it be he liked the look of me ?

He launched immediately into niggling tottering steps, full of breaks and hesitations,
quite impossible to follow. His eye wandered
slowly round the room and he took no notice
of her, pursuing his complicated course regardless of her stumblings.

In the hope of covering her incompetence by
a little friendly conversation, she ventured :

' You know, I don't think we know each
other's names, do we ? '

She tripped over his foot again.

' I know who you are.'

He sounded so casual, so nasal, not to say

bored, it was an effort to summon a coy smile
and ask :

' Who am I ? '

' Etty's young cousin, aren't you ? '

' Yes. How did you—— Oh, then, it is Etty
I saw. How extraordinary ! Does she know
I'm here ? Why hasn't she spoken to me ?
Did you come with her, then ? '

' Mm. With the Heriots. We're both staying with them.'

' I see. . . . Where is she now ? '

He jerked his head in the direction of the
staircase :

' Sitting out with your sister, I believe.
Having a good girl's gossip. Heu, heu, heu ! '
He uttered a dry little complacent laugh
through his nose. ' She told me I was to
dance with you.'

' I see. She pointed me out to you. . . .'

' Mm.'

What pleasure, what comfort, to have sat
with Kate and Etty for a quarter of an hour,
gossiping and giggling. But they hadn't included her. Going off together, Etty leaning
over the banister, shaking her head, flourishing
an arch little hand at him. Run along now,

you're not wanted. Go and dance with a nice girl. Look, there's another cousin of mine wall-flowering over there—go and console her. Be kind to her now. She's very young. . . . And then to Kate : Come on, my lamb. We mustn't waste a minute. Now, tell me *everything*. And upstairs they'd run, hand in hand, to have their secrets and be grown up together . . . just as in old times, playing Let's run away from Olivia.

Complicated emotion sharpened her voice, made her say suddenly :

'She told you to dance with me, so you did.'

'That's right. Heu, heu, heu ! Must obey orders, mustn't we ? '

'It was very kind of you both.' (What am I saying ? What's the matter with me ?) 'You really shouldn't have bothered.'

His eye fell on her for a second, infinitesimally disconcerted. 'Oh well, heu, heu, heu ! It's not exactly a hardship. What ? '

And he gave her hand a lingering squeeze.

I see what it is ; he's most awfully conceited. He thinks it's marvellous for me to be dancing with him. The squeeze is an extra special

favour. . . . Yet all the same, in spite of herself,
she felt a faint impulse to respond to it. It
was something personal, it must mean he
wasn't altogether bored.

In her new recklessness she said :

' Are you a friend of Etty's, then ? '

' Friend of Etty's ? Lord, yes. Known her
for years.'

' What heaps of friends she's got, hasn't
she ? '

' Mm. She's a popular little party.'

He sounded comfortable, complacent, possessive.

' Everybody falls in love with her, don't
they ? '

' Mm ? Well, I don't know about that. Heu,
heu ! . . .' His laugh was not so smooth.
' What makes you think so ? '

' Well, she's so attractive, isn't she ? ' She
paused and added : ' As a matter of fact, it's
what I gathered from what she tells me.'

' Oh, she tells you, does she ? . . .'

He was silent for a few moments, and then
said disagreeably :

' You're all alike, you girls. Just a lot of
scalp-hunters. Sitting round and counting

your scalps and bragging. But two can play at that game. Don't you forget that.'

She said awkwardly :

' I don't know anything about it.'

' Don't you ? Well, take my tip.'

She felt his uneasiness, his jealous hostility and suspicion reaching out beyond her, addressing itself to the tormenting image of Etty ; wondering : Does she give me away ? . . . and saw that he wished to marry Etty—and that he was not going to be able to. Then, in spite of his conceit, sooner or later he would be disconsolate. Failure would be bound to pierce his thick skin in the end. What would he do and say then ? She felt an anticipatory pity for him, wished to undo the effect of her indiscretion, to reassure him . . . make him stop disliking me so much. She said soothingly:

' I'm sure Etty doesn't do that. She never brags. Most girls are supposed to give away secrets, aren't they ? But Etty never does. That's why everybody tells her everything.'

He looked straight at her for a moment, some expression struggling in the blankness of his eyes, almost as if he might be going to

speak, to say something real. But in the end,
all he said in a patronizing way was :

'You're an unsophisticated damsel, aren't
you ? '

What does he mean by that? She was silent.

'Etty's all right,' he said in his former smug
voice. 'She's a sweet.'

'Yes.'

She was getting a little more used to his
steps, and managed now to totter and start off
again on the right foot without actual collapse
at least three times out of every four. His eye
continued to wander slowly round, and hoping
to have hit on a topic of interest to him, she
said :

'Which do you think the prettiest girl in the
room ? '

He looked at her quizzically, laughing heu,
heu, heu behind his silly little moustache.

'Aha ! Comparisons are odious, my sweet.'

He thinks I'm fishing. . . . A dark blush
raced over her.

He said in a fruity languishing voice, opening
his eyes at her :

'And is this her very very first dance ? '

'Yes, it's my first dance.'

' Having a wonderful time, are you ? Mm ? Heu, heu ! You jeunes filles are rather pets.' He squeezed her hand again. ' Such fun . . .'

' I'm not so young as all that. At least I don't feel it.'

' Old enough to be treated with proper respect, aren't you ? '

' Yes.'

' Heu, heu ! You're rather a joke, aren't you ? A nice one.'

Now that he had become personal, it was worse than before, after all—more sterile, more depressing. Because it isn't that he likes me. He thinks I like him so awfully.

The band stopped, and he relinquished her with indifference.

' Sorry I danced so badly,' she said.

She saw Peter in the passage, standing propped against the wall. She smiled at him as she went by. He clutched at her arm :

' You deserted me,' he said. ' Why did you ? '

' I didn't.'

His eyes looked very odd and his lip was quivering.

' Yes, you did. You know you did. And I know why you did.'

He shook her arm, his fingers hard and painful. She was dumb, staring at his white face. What's the matter with him? . . . What have I done? . . .

He swung round violently, as if he couldn't bear the sight of her. There was nothing to do but leave him. Feeling dazed, she rejoined her partner, who had walked on a few paces and was standing waiting with ostentatious disapproval.

' Who's that cad? ' he said, drawling through his nose.

' His name is Peter Jenkin.' After a bit she added : ' He isn't one.'

' Isn't what? '

' What you called him.'

' Oh, isn't he? Heu, heu ! Sorry I put my foot in it. Didn't know he was a pal of yours.'

He sounded teasing and nasty.

' There's something wrong with him.'

She felt terribly worried.

' Oh, there's something wrong with him all right. Heu, heu ! '

§ 9

Etty came down the stairs with Kate, greeted her joyfully, compensating for previous neglect with little pats and confidential whispers.

' Enjoying yourself, my lamb ? *How* nice you look with your hair up. *What* fun to be all at a dance together. Tell me, how did you get on with my old Podge ? He's rather a lamb, isn't he ? And dances so divinely. Hasn't he got an attractive *mind* ? Sort of whimsical and subtle.'

The dream was beginning to deepen. One could only agree and smile, eager, dissembling.

Etty put a hand on his shoulder and danced away with him ; her slender legs, her little feet slipping into the broken steps with perfect ease ; following him delicately, rhythmically. She thought she heard him drawl :

' That little cousin of yours is quite a sweet, but she needs teaching.'

She thought she saw Etty nod in a sprightly way and move her lips . . . uttering some cold, some casual, uncaring betrayal.

She stood with Kate by the door for a few minutes longer, smiling and smiling. Then

Tony Heriot came and took Kate away. And she went on standing there and smiling.

Was it dancing lessons he meant—or something about—how to behave?

My dress is crude, I'm unsophisticated, I need teaching.

I must go back to Peter and put it right with him.

§ 10

' You know,' she said kindly, ' I didn't desert you—you deserted me.'

She tried to make him look at her, but he wouldn't.

' I thought you wanted to get rid of me,' she said, smiling.

Still he said nothing, and scowled at the floor.

' Well, I'm awfully sorry.' She sighed. ' I didn't mean anything.'

He said with extreme bitterness :

' I know they put you up to it. That damned old bitch and her half-wit satellites. What did they say about me ? I know they've got their knife into me. What did they say ? '

'They didn't say anything,' she said, bewildered. 'They didn't mention you.'

'I suppose you expect me to believe that?' Suddenly he seized her hand. She saw that tears were pouring down his face. 'Look here, you ask him . . .' he quavered. 'Ask him if he meant it.'

'Ask whom?' She clasped his hand, longing to help, completely mystified.

'Are you my friend?'

He looked at her, frowning, anxious, tearful, like a child.

'Of course I am. Of course.'

'Promise to be my friend.'

'I promise.'

'They all hate me. They always have.'

'I'm sure nobody hates you.'

'I tell you everybody does,' he said angrily. 'They simply loathe me. I'm the loneliest beast in the world.'

Best not to contradict him. He's not himself at all. Kate'll say I'm making it up when I tell her. . . . Men are much, much queerer than I imagined.

He repeated :

'Ask him why he was so beastly to me. Will you? I'll wait here. Go on. I'll wait here.'

'But I don't know who you mean. I'm sure nobody meant to be beastly to you. If you go on like this I shall cry too.'

After a silence, he said, more calmly, with a sort of aggrieved dignity : 'Yes, he did. He meant to be absolutely foul and bloody.'

'Have you been having a quarrel ? '

'Yes. No. I don't know. We got into an argument. He simply began hurling insults at me.'

'Did he really ? '

'Yes, he was most frightfully rude.' He thought for a minute. 'He said I was drunk, among other things. The drink's absolutely foul anyway. So typical of the upper classes. Stingy beasts. I told him so.'

'Who is he ? '

'*I* don't know. . . . One of the footmen perhaps.'

He seemed thoroughly confused.

'Look here,' she said earnestly, still holding his hand. 'You go home. This isn't the right place for you. Honestly it's not. You'll be much happier if you go away. Will you ? '

She felt maternal, protective, certain she knew what was best for him.

228

'Why should I?'

But he didn't say it argumentatively.

'Go on,' she half insisted, half coaxed.

'These fools,' he said, looking about him.

Why did he go on about them like this? He seemed to have his knife into them terribly. His manner appeared to imply infinite disgust and contempt for all this sort of thing—houses, titles, people like the Spencers—what he called upper classes. Whereas oneself, one had always been led to believe they were very admirable, very desirable.

'Do go.'

'All right, I will.'

He turned and went away, without another word. He had forgotten again about limping, and walked rapidly, though perhaps a tiny bit unsteadily. She saw him go out of the front door.

§ 11

The sleek and brilliant beacon of Maurice's hair came bobbing through the crowd. Cool, quiet, practical, attentive, he glided up to claim her, and immediately sprang with her

into his usual brisk measure. He seemed somehow more definite than other people—as if his
eyes and ears were quicker, clearer. It was a
nice feeling to be with him again ; almost like
getting out into the fresh air.

The conversation with Peter immediately
became too unreal, too fantastic to think about.
She put it away in the back of her mind.

§ 12

The elderly gentleman with the thick white
wavy hair approached her. She had noticed
him before, dancing with the youngest girls in
the room one after the other; the girls drooping a little, pressed to his paunch.

' Would you be so very very kind as to spare
a dance for an old fogey ? '

' Oh yes, of course I will.'

' What ? You will ? Oh, how kind ! '

He clasped her to him and set off with slow,
rather laboured but elegant strides.

He repeated :

' How kind to spare a dance for old
Methuselah.'

' Oh, but you're not old.'

She gave him an encouraging smile. His skin was puckered and wrinkled, tortoise-like, under the chin, his cheeks puffy and veined with purple, his eyes a bit glazed and blood-shot. Otherwise he didn't look too bad. His hair was beautiful.

'What? Oh, come now—you're trying to flatter me—aren't you? . . . Not that I feel my age. Not a bit of it. Far from it.'

'It's what you feel that matters, isn't it?'

'Ah, very true, very true. What a clever little lady. You've hit the nail on the head this time. It's what you feel that matters. I feel as young as ever, and that's a fact. If the heart stays young, why, then, *you* stay young, whatever the calendar has to say about it—eh?'

'Yes, of course.'

Gathering impetus from this reflection, he crushed her to him and swung heavily, vigor-ously round on a corner. . . . 'Shall I tell you a secret? Eh?'

'Yes, do.'

She beamed at him, all attention.

'I only took up dancing again two years ago. Before that—ah, well—circumstances were different. I'd have said my dancing days

were done . . . over and done. . . .' He blew
a gusty sigh down her neck.

' Oh, really ? ' After a few more steps, she
added, ' And now you've started again ? '

' I have,' he said gravely. ' The ladies are
very kind to me—especially the young ladies.
They don't seem to mind dancing with me.
They don't object.'

' I should think not,' she said warmly.

He must have had a Great Sorrow, and put
it behind him. His voice was brave and
ringing.

' I must confess I had my qualms at first. I
thought the old machinery might creak a bit.
Ha ! Ha ! Ha ! ' He swung again, quite
wildly, to show how well the old machinery
was working. ' As a matter of fact I took a
few lessons on the quiet, just to get the hang
of this jazz, you know. I was very lucky in
my teacher. Doreen Delaval her name was.
A thoroughly cheery soul—you know, a real
jolly girl, as keen as mustard—pretty girl, too—
a lady, of course. Belonged to an old county
family. Fell on bad times, had to sell their
place up. This little girl Doreen she'd always
had a turn for dancing, so she pulled up her

socks and took to it for a living. Plucky thing
to do.'

'Does she manage to—to make a living all
right?'

'What? M'yes, yes. She's all right. She's
doing well.'

He was beginning to breathe a trifle heavily.
She ventured :

'Just say when you'd like to stop.'

'Stop? Do you want to stop?'

'Oh no, rather not. I just thought perhaps
you might like to.'

'Not a bit of it. I can dance all night and
feel the better for it. And that's a fact.'

'Can you really?'

She looked up at him admiringly, for he was
still a bit put out, suspicious.

'Yes, and I don't lie late abed next morning.
I don't coddle myself—never have. That's
what's kept me fit. But of course if you want
a rest . . .'

'Oh *no*. I'd much rather go on.'

'Afraid I don't know many of these new-
fangled steps. I don't get much practice.'

'Oh, I don't mind. I'm not a bit well up
in them either.'

But this wasn't the right answer. A silence
ensued, and she amended :

' As a matter of fact, you dance beautifully.
You're so frightfully easy to dance with.'

' What ? Do you think so ? Ah, I'm afraid
you're a flatterer. What ? Aren't you ? '

' Not at all.'

Curious : he had a sort of family likeness to
Major Skinner ; but—owing perhaps to the
loftier moral tone—he was somehow more cloy-
ing, more slippery ; and far more uneasy and
exacting.

' Ah, well, I dare say some folk would call
me an old fool.'

' Why should they ? '

' What ? Undignified, you know. Making
myself ridiculous.'

'How absurd. I'm sure nobody could think so.'

' What ? D'you think it's absurd ? Well, so
do I. But folk are apt to get in a groove as they
grow older, you know. They lose their resilience,
their elasticity. Their horizons contract.'

' I expect they forget they were young themselves once.'

' Ah, that's it.' He was delighted. ' They
forget. They get narrow-minded.'

234

'Narrow-minded people are such a bore. I don't think it matters what they say. They're not worth bothering about. Where I live I shock some of the old frumps dreadfully because I go for walks without my hat on.'

'Oh, so you're unconventional too, are you? Then you and I'll get on like a house afire. I thought we should. We've got a lot in common. I felt it directly I saw you.' He pressed her to him, sighed richly. 'The gods were good to me, little lady. They granted me a spirit that can never grow old. Whatever they denied me, they granted me that. I suppose that's why you young folk don't seem to mind my company.' He paused, but this time she failed him and remained silent, and soon he added with another, thinner sigh: 'All the same, one feels lonely sometimes.'

'I hope you're not lonely,' she said politely.

'What? Lonely? Ah well, I can't complain. Life can be very rich in spite of everything. One can be alone and yet not lonely, can't one? One has one's philosophy.'

She tried to give him a look of bright interest, but it was getting harder. He does need so much bolstering up.

'All the same, there are times when one longs for real companionship—for the touch of a vanished hand——' He lowered his voice to add : ' I lost my dear wife three years ago. We were everything to each other.'

What was it in the way he said this that froze the springs of sympathy ? Perhaps the way he dropped his voice ; or a sort of glibness, as if there were a crack, an unsound place concealed. . . . But of course it must have been a terrible grief.

' I'm so sorry. How awful for you.'

' Thank you. I knew you were sympathetic. Your voice told me so. Gentle and low, an excellent thing in woman.' He pressed her again. ' Ah, sympathy's a wonderful gift.'

The band stopped. He released her, clapped enthusiastically, mopped his face. He was perspiring freely.

' Ah, that was splendid—splendid. Now what about an ice ? Eh ? ' He looked at her roguishly. 'That 'ud slip down nicely, wouldn't it ? Come on now. Let's see how many we can account for. I'll take you on ! '

She followed him, wanly simpering. His schoolboy spirits weren't infectious.

236

§ 13

Tony said :

' Look here, don't you ever ride ? '

' No,' said Kate. ' I never do. When I was very small we had a pony. But the truth is—since the war we haven't been able to afford anything much.'

' How sickening for you. You would so love it.'

' I'm sure I would. It's always been one of the things I wanted most—to have a horse of my own.'

He said with his quick engaging diffidence :

' You'd look corking on a horse. You're simply made for it.'

' Am I ? '

She smiled, looking over his shoulder with shining unseeing eyes.

' I could teach you in no time.'

' Do you think you could ? '

' I know I could.' He continued eagerly : ' And I could mount you too. I've got the very horse for a beginner. An old mare of my father's, as comfortable and quiet as anything. . . . Why not ? '

237

' Well, for one thing I haven't any clothes.'

' Oh, bother clothes. We'll find you a pair of breeches.'

' All right. I'd love to.'

' I'll take you a few times round our big field for a start, and then as soon as you've got confidence we could go up on to the downs.'

' Oh, how glorious ! '

They looked at one another, radiant.

§ 14

Dance after dance with an old fogey. Three running now, pressed to his paunch. It seemed as if it might go on for ever. Not even Reggie to the rescue. Reggie must be at the buffet with the Martins. Neither he nor they had appeared upon the floor for a considerable time. No hope, no help. Programme a blank right on till Number 19, and that seemed now distant and improbable as a dream.

His name was Mr. Verity. He spoke of the little shack he had recently acquired in the vicinity ; of the wonder of the sunsets viewed from his study window. He mentioned his best friends his books, and quoted more than once from the Poet. Gather ye rosebuds, he said. Also, Then come kiss me sweet and twenty. Also, Si joonesse savvy. He asked her if she would take tea one day with a lonely old man ; his housekeeper, dear devoted old soul, would make her welcome. He talked a good deal too about people with titles whom he fished and shot with.

Her senses shrank away from him. They seemed to shout their frantic distaste into his heedless, his leathery ear. I don't like you. I don't like touching you. I hate dancing with you. I can't bear you. She gave up smiling ; almost gave up answering. Her face set stiffly, in utter dejection. Next dance I'll say I'm booked and go and hide in the cloakroom. But he'll know it's an excuse. It'll hurt his feelings. He'll go away and think, I'm a lonely old man. Oh, help ! help ! Will no one help ?

As she accompanied him for the fourth time towards the ballroom, Marigold appeared suddenly from nowhere, caught at her arm ; whisked her aside, drew her far away without a word to him or a backward look.

' I thought you needed rescuing.'

' Oh, I *did!* You angel ! '

She clasped Marigold's hand in pure relief and gratitude.

' I thought sudden tactics would be the most effictitious. . . . You did look downhearted.'

' I thought I'd never get away from him.'

' I know what he's like—the old octopus——' Her voice was harsh with contempt. ' He fished and fished for an invitation to this. He's our neighbour, worse luck. He's taken that cottage by the south gate. He tells every one Daddy and he were lads together at Cambridge, and that Daddy begged him to come and settle near him. I call him Johnny Walker. Did he ask you to tea ? '

' Yes. He did.'

' I thought as much. He's always trying that on. Mum thinks he's harmless, but of course he's not likely to be up to any of his tricks with her. They talk politics and county together, and he butters her up, and she thinks he's so sensible and so fond of young people and so picturesque and old-world with his white hair. In fact she was quite umbrageous with me when I called him a dirty old man. But of course Mum's hopeless. She thinks

240

virgins are sacred to all men—you know, all
the Tennyson flower stuff. Of course he's the
most infernal snob too, but she can't see that.
Still, I must admit he's quite different with
the elderly ones. You wouldn't know him.
It's the young ones that rouse him—especially
the ones in their teens.'

' How queer. . . . Have you been to tea with
him ? '

' Catch me. He did try it on once, but I
said could I bring my governess, so he changed
the subject.'

' What d'you suppose he'd do ? '

' Oh, fumble about a bit, I expect—you
know, feel your muscle and mess about with
your hands pretending he's a fortune-teller,
and measure how tall you were against him—
that sort of feeble pawing. It's a sort of disease
old men get, I believe.'

' Yes, I think it must be.'

' They go native. Honestly it's a warning.
Did he tell you he'd got a grown-up son and
daughter ? '

' No, he didn't. He kept on hinting he was
all alone in the world.'

' He would. But he's got two children, and

they won't live with him. Mum thinks it's
this modern selfishness, but I bet the trouble
was he was too sprightly for them. Fancy
having a lasciverous old father prodding and
stroking every girl you brought into the house.
Mine's not like that—not yet, anyway. Is yours?'

' Oh no. Not in the least.'

Dad prodding young girls. . . . Olivia
giggled.

' Though he adores a mild flirt with the
pretty ones.'

' I don't think mine even does that,' said
Olivia, after reflection.

She saw Johnny Walker standing alone by
the ballroom door, pretending not to watch
them out of the corner of his eye. He knows
we're talking about him. How was it that
Marigold, so sheltered, so well brought up,
knew so much, in such a shrewd, cynical,
coarse-grained way, about the facts of life?—
had on the tip of her tongue the best sort of
snub for a tiresome old man, so that he knew
it was no go, so that he feared her? Whereas
oneself, one would never know what to say,
one never spotted hidden motives, swallowed
any story, trusted everybody, would very

likely land oneself in a mess one day. . . . Even
now, seeing him furtively watch Marigold's
pert expressive face, feeling him brood sheep-
ishly over the ungracious, the wanton, flouting
way they'd left him in the lurch, yet not dare
to approach them, feeling the sickly collapse
of his self-esteem, even now she was tempted
to reassure him somehow, apologize, show him
she was sorry. For it was Major Skinner all
over again—the painfulness of seeing an old
white-haired person humiliated before youth,
ashamed of wanting the thing he wanted.
He'd never get it. It was too late. He was
old and done for. How his heart must ache.
. . . Oh dear ! I wish I could want to comfort you. . . . She saw the faintly stricken expression on his face. He stood there repre-
senting the pathos, the indignity of being old ;
of the dancing days being done. Oh, maidens !
he cried in vain. He wouldn't dare ask any
more of them to dance to-night. Soon he
would creep off home. And Marigold had
done this to him without an instant's com-
punction or compassion . . . out of kindness
to, pity for, oneself ? . . . out of pure malice
and scorn for him ? A strange impulse, a

curious action—one of Marigold's. Why, whence, out of her new estrangement and excitement, had she noticed, and darted ?

' There's Rex waiting for me. I must fly. Are you enjoying yourself ? Have you had lots of partners ? '

' I haven't got very much more booked,' admitted Olivia. ' Only Number Nineteen.'

' Oh, you must fill up or he'll pounce again.' She gave a chuckle. ' Who d'you fancy ? Oh, there's Timmy Douglas. He's so sweet. He's my favourite man—almost—no, quite. He's sure not to be full up, poor darling. When his wife's dancing with some one else, he mostly just stands and waits. Come on, I'll introduce you.'

She saw, against the wall inside the ball-room, a young man, tall, pale, standing and waiting. He seemed to be smiling ; but on a closer view, it seemed not to be a smile after all. It was a queer taut set of the muscles round his mouth.

' He's a marvellous dancer,' said Marigold. ' You'd never dream he's——' She lowered her voice abruptly as they came near to him, and her last words were inaudible—stone something or other, it sounded like.

She cried :

' Timmy, hullo ! '

He had been looking towards her without recognition, but now his face lit up faintly.

' Marigold ? '

His voice had an edge·of question. He put his hand out in a wooden way, straight in front of him, and she clasped it in both her own.

' Timmy darling, I meant to come and find you ages ago. But I've been so whizzed about all the evening. Are you happy ? '

Her voice had a softer, more caressing note than one had ever heard before. He answered with not quite convincing enthusiasm :

' Yes, rather.' He waited a moment, then said hesitatingly : ' When can I have a dance, Marigold ? '

Then he waited again. His face became suddenly patient and listening. His voice was patient too, quiet, flat, rapid. He didn't look at her.

' Oh, darling ! I'm so full up. Isn't it sickening ? '

' That's bad luck—for me.'

Patient and cheerful.

' Timmy, I've brought Olivia Curtis to dance

with you.' He turned his head slightly and sharply ; out came his hand again. His eyes, upon which the full lids constantly opened and fell with a long spasmodic movement, were opaque, navy blue in colour, like those of a new-born baby.

' How d'you do ? '

The smile that wasn't a smile tightened the muscles of mouth and cheek.

' Olivia's very nice with her practically black hair turned round each side of her face in a plaited bun, and a red dress.'

Had she really said that ? The dream had come on again.

' I must fly, Timmy darling. I'll come back later, for sure and certain.' Brushing past Olivia, her fingers clung for a second on her arm, she whispered fiercely : ' *Did you hear ?* He's——' but again the last word, sharply muted, was lost as she fled on.

He stood without moving, his head a little bent as if he were listening to her going. He said in his pleasant flat voice :

' She's got more vitality than half a dozen ordinary people. She just leaves it in the air around her, wherever she's been.'

It was quite true. It was the secret of Marigold, that one had never been able to define. She agreed, pleased, surprised. It was an unusual thing to say.

'It's a marvellous possession,' he said. 'The only gift I'd trouble a fairy godmother for. If you've got it, you can't be beaten. What's more, you make other people imagine they can't be. . . .'

He smiled now, a real smile, but faint. He himself looked as if he lacked vitality. He was pale and thin, rather worn-looking. He had beautifully-cut long delicate features and straight light hair growing rather far back above a high frail prominent forehead. He gave an impression of scrupulous cleanness and neatness.

'Would you care to dance?' he said. 'I'm afraid I'm apt to barge into people. The room's pretty full, isn't it?'

'Rather full.'

She looked at him, puzzled. Once again he had turned an obvious statement into a question. She looked at him, and in a sudden stab and flash of realization, saw him as one isolated, remote, a figure alone in a far place. He was——

' However, if you don't mind steering a bit. I generally manage more or less.'

He stood and waited, crooking his right arm ready to receive her. She saw that he was blind. She led him out on to the floor, and they started to dance.

I'll guide you, I'll look after you. Depend on me. . . . Blinded in the war? There wasn't a scar—nothing to proclaim it—only the opaque swimming irises between the heavily-twitching lids ; and the set of his face. His hand, holding hers, vibrated as if it had a separate, infinitely sensitive life—long fingers, exquisite nails. He'll guess what I'm like from my voice, from touching me. What will he guess? They say blind people always know, you can't deceive them.

They collided badly with another couple, who looked at him in cold surprise.

' Sorry,' he said pleasantly, ' my fault.'

He waited while they moved on. She saw the girl's face alter suddenly, not in pity, but in a look of avid curiosity. She whispered something to her partner, they both turned to stare at him. How dare they stare like that! . . .

' I'm sorry,' she said. ' I never saw them.

You dance so beautifully, I just forgot to steer.'

He looked a little bit pleased.

' We used to dance a lot at the place I was— St. Dunstan's, you know. I don't do much in that line now. Molly's awfully keen on it. I wish she got more.'

' Is that your wife ? '

' Yes, she's dancing, I think—I believe she's dancing with Rollo Spencer.'

' Oh yes, I see her.'

She saw Rollo quite close to them, dancing with a shortish person in rather a dowdy royal-blue dress—quite commonplace, quite insignificant. She had a good deal of straight brown hair, inclined to wispiness at the sides, blue eyes, some moles on her face, a weather-beaten skin without powder or make-up. There was nothing one could say about her, think about her. Olivia searched in vain for traces of spiritual intensity, renunciation, suffering, such as might fitly mark the face of one devoting, sacrificing all to a blind husband. She looked sensible, capable, her eyes clear and hard. Rollo must be dancing with her out of niceness. She glanced at her husband and his partner, but only for a minute, without apparent interest. I suppose you get used—I suppose you soon get used. . . . It all depends how you let yourself think about it. Even now, already, it was getting quite easy to behave towards him as his simplicity, his utter non-assumption of the role of martyr, his rather negative, low-pitched but unforced cheerfulness demanded—to treat him as one like other men. It was as if he were tacitly demonstrating : You see, it isn't a tragedy at all. You needn't be sorry for me. . . . Yet the first image persisted in the background of her mind : a figure in its essence far apart.

' The Spencers are most frightfully nice, aren't they ? ' he said. ' They've been most awfully decent to us.'

' Do you live near ? '

' Oh yes, I'm one of their tenants. We've got that little house beyond the church—about a mile away. Do you know it ? Cherry Tree Cottage it's called—and it's actually got a cherry tree too.' His voice was more lively now. He liked talking about his house. ' Lady Spencer's helped us no end—Sir John too—— We're chicken farmers. Thanks to

them, we've worked up quite a big connection
—that's the right term, isn't it ? We supply
all the eggs and poultry for the house too.'

' Do you like doing it ? '

' Oh yes, I like it all right. There's more in
chickens than you'd think.' He smiled. ' I
used to think they were the most ghastly
feeble animals. If anybody'd told me I'd be
keeping them for a living, I'd have—well, I
don't know what. As a matter of fact, I
wanted to be an architect—that's what I was
keen on. But if you really take up a thing
you can't help getting interested—don't you
think ? '

' Oh yes, I quite agree.'

She searched his face—it was placid ; his
voice, now he was surer of his ground, equable
and very young-sounding. How did one look
after chickens when one was blind ?

' Molly's awfully keen on it, luckily. In fact
it was she who got the whole thing going.
She's awfully practical and good at running
things. She does most of the dirty work, really.
It keeps us busy. It's all jolly scientific these
days, a proper chicken farm, I can tell you.'

' Is it ? How frightfully interesting.'

' Molly's always lived in the country, but I'm a London bird. I didn't think I'd like it at first, but I've got quite used to it. I must say one does feel better—don't you think ? Sort of more peaceful. It's nice for the infant too, to be brought up in the country. She loves animals. She's got a pet duckling that follows her everywhere.'

His smile spread clear over his face.

' Have you got a little girl ? '

' Rather.'

' How old is she ? '

' Getting on for two. She runs about like anything, and chatters all day. She's pretty forward, I think.'

' What's her name ? '

' Elizabeth. Molly wanted Marjorie and I wanted Susan, so we split the difference with Elizabeth. It's a good name, don't you think?'

' Yes. I love the old English names.'

She was moved by his simple pride and pleasure in his possessions—his family, his farm, everything that told him he was a man with a background, a place in the world ; a successful grown-up man who had by his own labours established his security. But he looked so young to be a husband and father—not more than twenty-two. Molly didn't look nearly so young. Perhaps she'd been his nurse. Probably he'd never seen her. . . . He'd never see his daughter either. One must try not to let that seem too pathetic. It was the sort of thing that brought a too-easy sob in the throat. It doesn't matter, it doesn't matter really.

'Marigold rides over to see us pretty often,' he said. 'We look forward to that.' (It was queer really that Marigold had never mentioned him. . . . But she was so secretive.) 'She'd buck anybody up, wouldn't she? She's so frightfully amusing, isn't she? Really witty. . . . Otherwise it's a quiet life. Not that I mind. I play the gramophone a lot in the evenings. I like music awfully. But I wish Molly got out more. It's dull for her.'

She plucked up courage to say timidly :

' Do you—can you find your way about— fairly well in your house ? '

' Oh Lord, yes. Anywhere. Like a cat, you know. I see in the dark.' He smiled at his joke, adding mildly but emphatically :

Oh, Molly's not tied like that—not to that

extent. I can do pretty well everything for
myself.'

She saw him going up and downstairs,
dressing, undressing, feeding himself, patiently
listening to his gramophone, changing the
needle, walking over his farm, scattering grain
to the hens, painstakingly independent, giving
no trouble.

She murmured :

' I know—I'm sure—you're simply—— It's
so difficult to realize there's anything wrong.
I hadn't an idea.'

' Oh well,' he said equably, ' it's all a question of one's point of view, isn't it ? One's
taught not to—well, not to think of it as a
misfortune, you know.'

' When were you—how long ago——? '

' June 1918.' His voice was even. ' I went
out from school. I only had three months of
it. A sniper got me plunk behind the eyes.'

She was silent. War, a cloud on early
adolescence, weighing not too darkly, long
lifted. . . . A cousin in the flying corps killed,
the cook's nephew gone down at Jutland,
rumour of the death of neighbours' sons—
(that included Marigold's elder brother), and

among the village faces, about half a dozen familiar ones that had disappeared and never come back . . . and butter and sugar rations ; and the lawn dug up for potatoes (the crop had failed) ; and knitting scratchy mittens and mufflers ; and Dad being a special constable and getting bronchitis from it : that was about all that war had meant. And during that safe, that sheltered unthinking time, he had gone out to fight, and had his eyes destroyed. She saw him reel backwards, his hands on his face, crying : I'm blind . . . or coming to in hospital, not realizing, thinking it was the middle of the night. . . . Imagination stretched shudderingly towards his experience. She had a moment's dizziness : a moment's wild new conscious indignation and revolt, thinking for the first time : This was war—never, never to be forgiven or forgotten, for his sake.

I'd stay with you, I'd look after you. I'd be your eyes and show you everything. Oh— is she nice enough to you ? But if it was me, I'd be too sorry, I'd upset him. She's sensible, she's matter-of-fact, she takes it for granted. How dare she. . . . She keeps his life practical and orderly, keeps him cheerful. They've got a child. So he must love her. And it doesn't matter to him that she's not young or pretty. ... Yes, all his gratitude, all his solicitude were for her.

The band stopped.

' Thank you very much indeed,' he said. ' I'm just getting the hang of the room. It's jolly big, isn't it ? '

' Yes, very big, with big mirrors in the panels, and chandeliers. It's very bright—the light, I mean.'

' I can remember photographs of this house in some paper. I remember it quite well. It's a beautiful house. A perfect specimen, but just unconventional enough to have a character of its own.'

He stood in the middle of the room, thinking about it.

She said nervously :

' What would you like to do ? Shall we go and sit somewhere ? '

' Rather. Anything you like——'

' Would you like an ice—or anything ? '

' Yes, what about an ice ? A drink anyway— I could do with a drink.'

He laid his fingers on the tip of her elbow, and she led him to the dining-room. He walked with a light quick step straight on his course, his touch on her arm almost imperceptible ; not at all like one's idea of the shuffle and grope of a blind man. Only his head looked somehow vulnerable and wary. She felt important, self-assured, helping him, not shy or self-conscious in spite of people staring.

' Here's a beautiful armchair,' she said.

' Thanks.'

He lowered himself into it after a second's hesitation.

' Wait here, I'll get you a drink. What would you like ? '

' Oh, anything cool, thanks. I'm a teetotaller these days.'

Waiting at the buffet for orangeade, she watched him take out his silver case and a matchbox and light his cigarette, slowly and carefully. Then he smoothed his hair, adjusted his tie, brushed his sleeve, his shoulders. In case I've left any mark, powder, a hair or anything. He's afraid of looking slovenly, neglected, ridiculous, and not knowing it. That's why

he's neater, more polished up than anybody
else. He didn't smoke his cigarette, but let it
burn away between his long fingers. He sat
back, his head slightly bent, the muscles taut
in his face, waiting.

Now he looks like a blind man.

He was very easy to talk to. She chatted to
him without effort or embarrassment until the
next dance began, and his wife came strolling
towards them. She walked with her square
shoulders hunched. The skin of her neck and
arms was rather rough and red, and her legs
were short, muscular, slightly bandy. She
looked like a hockey-playing cross-country-
striding person, in striking contrast to his
pallor, his elegant narrow-hipped length.

'Hullo!' she said. Her voice was rather
rough too, with a twang in it.

He stirred without lifting his face.

'Oh hullo, Molly!' He added politely to
Olivia: 'Can I introduce my wife?'

She smiled, meeting Olivia's shy and eager
beam. Her smile was limited, but direct and
pleasant, and her eyes were nice too, a clear
bright blue.

Reggie was approaching. He looked a little

congested about the face. He mustn't meet
Timmy.

' Good-bye,' she said, and walked away.

She heard him say after a moment :

' Has she gone ? '

It was just a question. No suspicion, regret,
or relief in it. No interest.

§ 15

At last the cloakroom. Number 19 was very
near now. The next dance. I must prepare
myself and be in order. The thick carpet, the
rose colours, the lit objects of crystal and silver,
all these in their soft silence received her re-
assuringly. The elderly woman in attendance
welcomed her with a friendly smile. It was
Marigold's old Nannie. She bent to look at
herself in the triple mirror on the dressing-
table, and thought that her face looked somehow smaller, more contracted than usual. It
had long ago stopped being flushed ; it was
pale now, with rings under the eyes. I'm tired.
It had been a tiring evening. No, I haven't
really enjoyed myself. Strained anxious hours,
hollow hours. But Archie will make up for

everything. I'll be able to say I've had a lovely time. She opened one of the crystal jars and dabbed powder on her nose. Then she put in a few more hairpins. Not that they were necessary. The plaits had weathered the evening quite unshaken. I wonder if that smell's gone off my hair. . . . Perhaps that's why I haven't got on better. She washed her hands in the crystal basin. Never do to offer a sticky hand to Archie. She glanced in the long mirror . . . so red, so definitely the reverse of well cut. And every one at home thought it was such a lovely frock. I shall never like it any more. She straightened the crumpled water-lily. This was Lady Spencer's own bedroom. Family photographs abounded. Rollo, Marigold and the elder son, the one who'd been killed, from infancy onwards ; and above the mantelpiece, pastel portraits of them all as children, romanticized, beautiful, unconvincing. In that majestic damask-hung bed slept Sir John and Lady Spencer every night, after putting on pyjamas and nightdress and brushing their teeth like anybody else.

A soothing voice remarked :
' You need a stitch, miss.'

'Oh, where?'

'Your hem's hanging a wee bit here at the back.'

'Oh dear, so it is. I remember I caught my heel in it getting up from the stairs.'

'I've got a needle handy. I'll just catch it up. It won't take a minute. If you wouldn't mind standing.'

She knelt on the floor, her grey head with its neat thin bun of hair bent above the needle, stitching swiftly, with soothing clicks of the thimble.

'Are you having a nice evening, miss?'

'Oh yes, thank you, lovely.'

'That's right. Miss Marigold looks well to-night, doesn't she?'

'Yes, she does. Her dress is so beautiful.'

'Yes, it's a lovely little frock. Not everybody's frock. She carries it off just perfect.' She stitched away. 'It's quite a job for me to realize she's out. It seems only yesterday she was sitting up in her pram in a little white fur cap and coat.'

'Yes, time does go quick.'

'The opinion seems to be she'll be a great success. I may be partial, but she does seem to put other young ladies in the shade.'

' Yes, she really does.'

' But it won't spoil her. Marigold's a nature you can't spoil. She's too open. She was always the same from a little thing. Such a happy disposition too. High-spirited. Of course she's got a will of her own . . . but so affectionate with it. There, that won't show, miss.'

She broke off her thread and got up off her knees, short, trim, sober, self-effacing in the respectable black silk and cairngorm brooch, the flat strong heels of service. She smelt of water and soap and clean ironed linen, of all the upstairs world where she moved alone, sewed, folded, washed and pressed. Upstairs was her place, while downstairs ran Marigold, her masterpiece, flying out from beneath her cherishing wing to certain happiness.

A plump fair girl in yellow burst into the room.

' Oh, Nannie angel, my stocking's exploded into ladders. What shall I do ? '

' Gracious, Miss Hermione. I can't mend that. You'll have to change.'

' Oh, Nannie, must I really ? '

' Yes, indeed, I can't do miracles. I'll pop

along with you and look you out another
pair.' She added in quite a scolding voice :
'You shouldn't wear your suspenders so
tight. I'm always telling Marigold the
same.'

One of the house-party ; one of the inner
circle, the initiated.

§ 16

Number 19 was finished. Archie was still
standing just outside in the passage, looking in
at the ballroom. He was still talking to some
other young men and laughing a lot. He'd
been there ever since the music began. First
it had seemed as if he must be waiting, with
gratifying punctuality. But they were clapping
for the first encore and still he stood there.
Surely he had seen her. His eye, vague and
rapid, had rested on her for a moment and
passed on. He seemed not to recognize her.
She moved to a better position for being
noticed. First she sat down, then she got up
and stood against the wall. She watched him,
in a panic, without seeming to watch him.
Her heart-beats grew so loud and rapid, she

felt she must choke. After the second encore she went out of the ballroom into the passage, walking right past him. He glanced at her quite blankly. He must have mistaken the number—he must. And it was impossible to go up to him because of all those others. It can't be true. It's too much to bear. How can I live if things like this are going to happen? I never thought about his mistaking—or forgetting—or cutting. It never occurred to me. What shall I do? . . .

On the table beside her were some cigarettes in a shagreen box. She took one with an unsteady hand and managed to light it. Once or twice she and Kate had surreptitiously cut one in half and smoked it up the schoolroom chimney, so she knew how it was done. She sat down and puffed feverishly, in short jerks, blowing out the smoke immediately and puffing again. She was shivering violently.

§ 17

Out of the corner of an eye she saw the others move away. Archie went on standing there alone, looking rather vacantly in front of him.

Despair nerved her. She crushed out the cigarette and went quickly up to him.

' Did I make a mistake ? '

She smiled feebly.

' Wha' ? '

His eyes had a queer fixed far-away look. His tie was a trifle crooked, his hair ruffled ; altogether slightly disintegrated, informal-looking.

' Wasn't that Number Nineteen ? '

' Was that Number Nineteen ? '

He hardly seemed to take in what she said.

' Didn't you—weren't we dancing it together ? '

' Were we ? '

' I thought so.'

He isn't going to apologize, to say : Please let's have the next one instead. The dream was at its darkest, most irresponsible, most threatening.

' Sorry,' he said suddenly in a blurred voice. ' 'Fraid I'm a bi'—— It's the heat. Isn't it fun, though ? Marvellous party. Never laughed so much in my life.'

He began to laugh again, quite suddenly. She stood beside him wondering what to do next. He stopped laughing and looked at her with heavy fixity, took her arm, began to feel and press it, stroke it up and down with his hot fingers.

She took a breath and said :

' You know we've met before. I remember you ever so well. At a party here. When we were children.'

He said loudly :

' I don't remember when we were children.'

He let her arm drop.

' You had a broom and swept the floor.'

' Swept the floor, did I ? What on ear' for ? '

' I don't know.'

She heard the foolish echo of her own voice, like a tin tray clattering downstairs. She felt his obscure momentary interest in her stray off hazily, leaving her stranded, sheepish, snubbed with her misplaced advances, her untimely reminiscences.

She left him and went away.

§ 18

Tony said :

' I say, are you really off to Paris in the New Year ? '

' Yes, really.'

' What on earth do you want to do that for ? '

He had lost his diffidence. His conversation had the same kind of ease and joyful assurance as his way of holding her while they danced. She was so absolutely—so absolutely different.

' Well, I suppose I've got to be educated.'

' Why have you ? This fuss about education's all bunk. Being stuffed up with a lot of old junk out of books that'll never be any use to you and just addles your head if you do want to use it for anything sensible. Not that I'm speaking from experience. I never did a stroke at school or Oxford.'

They laughed delightedly. He went on :

' But I hate these frightfully learned people, don't you ? They don't get any fun out of life. They're all made of sawdust. You won't get like that, will you ? Promise.'

' I promise I won't.'

' I don't think you will, I must say.'

She had told him about the professor's family. She couldn't pretend with him, or keep things back.

' Of course it's fun to go abroad, though,' he said. ' If I could, I'd spend half of every year travelling.'

' Oh, so would I. I want to travel more than anything else in the world.'

' Do you ? '

' I seem to want so many things. They always tell me I'm so discontented and difficult to please.'

' I think you're absolutely right. I think we ought to be discontented at our age, otherwise we'll never get anywhere. My family think I'm awfully idle and easy-going, but I'm awfully—well, ambitious, I suppose, really.'

' Are you ? So am I.'

' One's family never know anything about one, do they ? '

' No, never.'

That was true. Not even Olivia—really.

' It's funny,' he said. ' I feel I've known you ages.'

' I know. I feel the same.'

After a silence she said :

' I wonder what you want ? '

' All sorts of things. . . . I wonder what *you* want ? '

' All sorts of things.'

They smiled dreamily. After another silence he said :

'If I hopped over for a week-end, would they allow me to take you out?'

'Oh! Oh, I'm sure they would. They'd have to.'

'I haven't been over for two years. I'd like to see it again. April's the best time—Easter. Honestly, it's corking in Paris round about then—the Bois and the plane trees coming out, and everything looking so clean and sort of spacious. Last time I was over there, I wandered about all day by myself, exploring —over the other side of the river. I'd love to do it again. With you.'

'Couldn't you come at Easter? I shan't be coming home till the summer.'

He said quietly, in a tone of suppressed excitement:

'Right. I will. If you're sure you'd like me to.'

She answered, almost under her breath:

'Yes, I would.'

They were silent, seeing themselves walking together beneath a blue and white Easter sky, down strange exciting sunny streets and under budding trees.

§ 19

The rain must have stopped a long time ago. A small wind had sprung up, but the air was mild, the waning moon flying crooked above the trees, shredded over with thin travelling rags of cloud. Olivia stood on the terrace and looked down over the lawn to the far-stretching wooded park. It was light enough to see the shape of a cedar in the middle distance, the paved pattern of the sunken garden beneath the terrace wall, the outline of the stone figure of the fountain pouring water from a shell, arms lifting it above the shoulder, head curved towards it. She saw the glinting stream running between the garden and the park. The spaces of sky and lawn were broad and peaceful. Trees, water, moonlight made up their own cold world, unalterable, infinitely detached from humanity. It was like dying for a bit to be out here. Living is going on on the other side of the wall, but I've left it. I don't want it. I hate it ; it hates and rejects me. I forget and am forgotten. I'm nothing.

Somebody was coming up the flight of steps

from the garden to the terrace. A man's figure appeared at the top and threw away a cigarette. He stood a few minutes, surprised, uncertain, seeing her straight ahead of him. Then he came sauntering towards her.

' Hullo ! ' he said.

It was Rollo.

' Hullo ! '

' What are you doing out here ? '

' I came out to get cool. It's hot in there, isn't it ? '

It was quite an effort to speak to him ; like coming back from being dead. She felt herself rooted to the ground and very calm, not embarrassed at all. Rather as if I might say anything. . . .

' Yes, it is. Though why you should feel it with the amount you've got on, I can't imagine. How'd you like to be boxed up like me ? '

' I get hot from nervousness. I get—you know—fussed, and then I feel like a boiled lobster.'

He received this in silence, looking at her with faint curiosity and amusement.

' Well, don't catch cold out here,' he said

finally. 'Oughtn't you to have something over you?'

'Oh no, it's lovely.'

She felt she could never have enough of this cool, washing, dark air all over her. She wanted it to soak into her, penetrate to the core. If I touch my arms the flesh is icy cold, but I don't feel it yet. I'm still burning inside. She stopped staring into the distance and looked up at him for the first time. He was a very handsome person. It ought to be most surprising and exciting to meet him like this alone on the terrace—a tremendous piece of good luck. But instead, she was taking it all for granted, as one did in dreams.

'I have met you before, haven't I?' he said.

'Yes, but you wouldn't remember me. You came into the schoolroom once when we were having tea with Marigold, after the dancing class. You stayed and had tea with us. You and Marigold played guitars and sang.' (What an evening that had been!)

'Of course. Then I do remember you. I knew I'd seen you somewhere. It's been bothering me all the evening.'

She glanced at him. He seemed to mean it.

Because of something wrong with me—queer ?
. . . No. It wasn't meant unflatteringly.

'But I've forgotten your name,' he said.

'Olivia. Olivia Curtis. Why does one
always feel silly telling one's own name ? '

'Olivia's a beautiful name.'

Their voices dropped into the air one after
the other with an impersonal lost sound, as if
they reached one another from a distance ; yet
the sense of isolation seemed to enclose them
together in a kind of intimacy. His voice was
deep and rounded, both vigorous and lazy.
He was tall, heavily built, with dark blue eyes
set apart above high cheekbones, and a full
well-cut mouth and chin, rather like Archie's.

She said :

'I've seen you dancing with somebody very
beautiful.'

He didn't answer for a moment, then said
rather flatly :

'Oh yes. Isn't she ? '

'What makes it different from other faces ?
You think when you look at her : This is a
face. Everybody else has got a bad imitation.'

He smiled.

'I believe the women in her family have

been beauties for generations. It's queer how it goes on sometimes.'

'What's her name ? '

'Nicola Maude.'

'Nicola Maude. Is she a famous beauty ? '

'I suppose she will be. She's only just appeared. She's been kept very dark down in Devonshire all her life. So she's making what's called a sensation.'

'Does she like it ? '

'I suppose she does. Any girl would, wouldn't she ? '

'I should think so. I know I would. It's one of my pet dreams—to walk into a room and everybody gasp.' She smiled. 'And that must really happen to her. How extraordinary ! What's she like ? '

'Awfully young and shy. Awfully quiet. I believe she just likes the country, and dogs and horses and all that sort of thing. She's not a bit spoilt. However, I suppose she soon will be.'

'What does she talk about ? '

'She doesn't talk. Hardly opens her mouth.'

'I suppose she feels it's enough to look. As much as any one could expect.'

' I suppose she does.' He laughed and added rather moodily : ' Oh, I don't know. I dare say she's as stupid as an owl.'

' It would be nice to think that—nice for one's envy, I mean. But I don't think she's stupid.'

' Oh, you don't . . .' Again he looked at her with curiosity and amusement.

' It's so much more sensible to keep quiet— but it needs so much strength of mind. I can't talk either, but I do. All the things I say seem to come wrong. I just feel more and more idiotic. I was thinking just now—I'd much better give it all up.'

Her voice quavered, suffused with tears.

He said very kindly :

' Oh, cheer up ! Didn't you ever have a French governess that told you ce n'est que le premier pas qui coûte ?'

' Yes, I did.' She smiled.

' I wouldn't decide to retire from the world just yet.'

It was a nice consoling feeling to be teased by him.

' This is the first dance I've been to.'

' Well, it'll be the last unless you come along

in quickly.' He turned towards the terrace and whistled. 'I was just going to give the dogs a run. Poor chaps, they're like me : they hate having their habits upset. They've been howling in the gun-room all the evening.'

He whistled again.

' Doesn't everything seem bare in this light ? As if all the coverings had been pared down and drained away and just the bones left.'

' Mm.' He looked about him. ' I like it.'

' So do I.'

Two dogs, a Sealyham and a Cairn, came hopping briskly up the steps from the garden. He bent to pat them.

' Good boys. . . . Come on, we'll put them to bed in my father's little room. There won't be anybody there, and it's more homely for them.'

He led the way back to the verandah from which she had emerged, his feet crunching the gravel with a firm slow reassuring tread.

' Don't you like dances, then ? ' she said.

' Not much. I like a quiet life, I do.'

Again she noticed the touch of moodiness in his voice.

' So do I, I believe.'

He opened the glass door for her, and they were once more inside the house, walking down a passage.

' So do you, do you ? What sort of things do you like ? '

' Reading, mostly. And going for walks by myself. And talking to Kate—that's my sister.'

' What sort of books do you like ? '

' Any kind almost. I like poetry specially. The Brontës and Dickens are my favourite novelists, but I like Thackeray too, specially *Vanity Fair*—and George Eliot and Jane Austen. I don't like Scott.'

' Oh, don't you ? I rather enjoy a tussle with old Scott.'

' What are *your* favourite authors ? '

She hadn't felt so happy all the evening. Such an interesting, serious conversation.

' Mine ? Oh, I only truly love two books in all the world.'

' What are they ? '

' One's called *Tom Jones*. The other's called *Tristram Shandy*. Directly I finish one I start the other, and so on. . . .'

' I haven't read them. I must.'

277

He laughed.

'Yes, do. You'd enjoy them. At least I think so.' He looked at her quizzically. 'Come and have a look at my father's books. He's got some nice ones he keeps to himself.'

He opened a door in the passage and ushered her into a small room with high bookshelves round three sides of it ; and drawn up to the fire, a large armchair containing an elderly gentleman. Sir John himself, spectacles on nose, pipe in mouth, volume in hand.

'Hullo, Daddy. I'd no idea you were here. I was just going to make Toppy comfortable in your armchair. What are you up to ?'

Sir John took off his glasses and heaved a sigh.

'Absenting myself from felicity awhile.'

'Shirker !'

They looked at each other humorously.

'Your Aunt Blanche and I were having a game of chess, but she's retired to bed. Your mother won't allow me to go to bed, so I thought I'd have a bit of a sit down with a book and a pipe.'

'Here's another recluse,' said Rollo.

'Another recluse, is she ? Come and sit

down.' He pulled up another armchair. She sat down on the edge of it, blushing and smiling, her hands folded tightly in her lap, her feet tucked well back. 'Let me see . . . of course we've met before, haven't we?'

'Yes,' she said in a small voice. 'I'm a friend of Marigold.'

'Olivia Curtis, isn't it?' suggested Rollo helpfully.

'Oh yes, yes—Charlie Curtis's girl. Of course. Yes, yes.'

Nobody quite knew what to say, but they all smiled, feeling friendly and vaguely conspiratorial.

'And what can I do for you?' said Sir John. 'Cigarette? Whisky and soda?'

He looked at her with his mastiff look, and she suddenly saw he must have looked rather like Rollo once, before he grew stout, bald and heavily moustached.

'She's a great reader, Daddy.'

'A great reader, is she?'

'Yes. You can't catch her out. Every one of your pet classics.'

While Rollo drank a whisky and soda, Sir John showed her his first editions and other

treasures—volumes signed and inscribed by
Wordsworth, Byron, Dickens and other cele-
brities. It was all very interesting, very gratifying, but embarrassing too. She couldn't
think of any intelligent remarks. After a bit
she said :

' I must go now. I'm sorry I disturbed
you.'

' Not at all. Delighted to have your company. Honoured.' He made her a little bow.

She looked up at Rollo smiling. They were
so kind. This was what real people were like
after all, just as she had always imagined ; not
sinister, inexplicable, but friendly and simple,
accepting one pleasantly, with humour but
without malice, without condescension, criti-
cism or caresses. How extraordinary to be here
with them ; from being outcast, flung beyond
the furthest rim, to have penetrated suddenly
to the innermost core of the house, to be in
their home. The dancing, the people beyond
were nothing, a froth on the surface, soon to
be blown away. This, that she felt as she
stood between them, was the reality about the
house : kindness, tolerance, courtesy, family
pride and affection.

'Thank you very very much,' she said, gratitude swelling in her throat.

'Back to the giddy throng,' said Sir John. He laid his hand on his son's shoulder. 'You too, get along with you. When I was your age I thought nothing of getting through three collars a night.'

'I like it really,' said Olivia. 'It was only that my programme got a bit empty.'

'Shame!'

'Oh, it doesn't matter a bit. I don't mind now.'

'How's your father these days?' said Sir John, relighting his pipe.

'He's pretty well, thank you. Some days worse than others. It's his asthma. But he's always very cheerful.'

'Ah, I'm glad of that. It's very hard for an active man to be an invalid. Remember me very kindly to him, will you?'

'Yes, thank you, certainly I will.'

He'd be pleased.

'Your father's a very able man.'

She beamed at him from the door.

'Good-bye, Daddy. I'll leave the dogs with you. They're so miserable.'

Rollo shut the door, and they went on down the passage and came out into the hall. Archie appeared from the dining-room and came towards them. He called out :

'Rollo, I say, old boy, where's that girl ? I thought I was dancing with her.'

'What girl ? '

Rollo's voice was cool.

'That long white snaky one. The peach. She gave me the slip. I've been looking for her everywhere.'

'I shouldn't worry about her. I expect she's dancing with some one else.'

'Is she, by God ! Wha' she mean by playing a trick like that ? The bitch. I'll tell her so.'

He swung round, looking about him angrily, vacantly.

'I should hop off to bed if I were you.'

'No, I won't hop off to bed. Damn you, Rollo. Wha' d'you mean by saying a thing like that ? Eh ? Wha' d'you mean by it ? '

Rollo said mildly :

'I don't mean anything. I don't care what you do.'

He put his finger-tips on Olivia's elbow to
motion her on. Archie stood muttering, not
attempting to follow them.

'Silly ass,' said Rollo. He sounded a little
annoyed. 'I'll have to try and get him upstairs before the end, or there'll be——'

He gave a quick glance round, which she
understood ; hoping his mother hadn't seen.
But Lady Spencer was nowhere about ; only
one couple on the sofa had been staring. She
realized now, of course, what was the matter
with Archie. What a staggering thing . . .
What a terribly bad lot he must be in spite
of his fascination—quite gone to the dogs.
And to think I went up and spoke to him,
not realizing—— Shame flooded her at the
thought. So that's what people are like
when they're drunk. (Could it be that Peter
too . . .?) How lucky that Aunt Blanche,
his poor mother, had gone to bed and would
be spared the shameful sight.

They saw Nicola coming alone down the
stairs. She stood half-way down, looking about
her, then catching sight of Rollo, from what
seemed an immense distance, raised her hand
slowly, summoning him. The pose as she fell

into it assumed a static quality like sculpture. She kept her hand up, perfectly still. What was in her mind ? There was less of appeal than assurance in the deliberate gesture ; she knew he would come. He made an eager forward movement, then stopped, looking at Olivia, uncertainly, apologetically.

' I'm all right.'

She smiled at him.

' Are you sure ? '

He was still charming, solicitous for her.

' Of course I am, go on.' She nodded her head gaily, emphatically, eager for him to go where he wanted to go, where he belonged. ' Good-bye.'

'Good-bye.' He looked down at her with the utmost friendliness, hesitated, added suddenly : ' I'm so glad we met,' and went quickly away.

She watched him go across the room. What a dear . . . He was the sort of person every one would want to call on in emergencies. His shoulders, his step and voice told them he knew what to do. He would cope, without fuss or self-importance. He was resolute. She was filled with affection, with admiration for him. She watched him and Nicola meet at

the foot of the stairs and start to talk earnestly,
their heads close together. They do suit. . . .
She went away.

§ 20

The band hung out a little sign saying
Extra, and started to play a waltz. A good
many people had left, more were leaving. The
dance would soon be over now. It must be
very late, surely Kate would be thinking of
going soon. Kate's had a lovely time, I'm sure.
Looking round for her, she noticed the blind
man sitting by himself in the little room that
opened on the ballroom. Waiting for some
one? He sat beneath the lamp; yet she saw
suddenly, struck to the heart, he seemed to sit
in shadow. Light had vanished not from his
eyes alone but from his ruined brow and all
his being. He would never emerge again. She
saw how his young weak face was frozen, how
it was wrenched, compelled into unnatural
lines; so that it was a mask, a grotesque mask
of strength and patience. She saw him sitting
alone downstairs in his house, waiting, and the
doctor coming in to tell him it was all over—

he was a father. It was not—not what should have happened to him. His mating and begetting should have been otherwise ; and not yet. They'd wronged him, they'd abused him. That scene was blasphemous, a sin, a counterfeit of life bred from his murdered youth.

He mustn't go on sitting there alone. She went quickly to him and said, almost in a whisper :

' Hullo ! '

Without moving, he became suddenly alert. He said rapidly :

' Marigold ! '

' No, it's not Marigold,' she said softly, with regret.

' Oh ! . . . Miss Curtis. I didn't recognize your voice for a moment. Hullo ! '

She felt him hastily readjusting the disturbed mechanism of his composure. This was his difficult achievement, the method by which he lived. It mustn't fail him. His face was empty and cheerful again, his voice had returned to its usual light surface level. He'd been expecting Marigold, but it was quite all right—it didn't matter. He didn't want anything.

286

She said timidly :

' Shall I try and find her for you ? '

' Good Lord, no.   She must be fearfully busy.'

He didn't like having given himself away. He didn't want her to remind him of his little mistake.   After a pause he said lightly :

' Who's she dancing with, I wonder ? '

She looked.   It was the sleek dark boy, Rex, attractive, narrow-skulled, rat-skulled, whom she'd been with a good deal during the evening.   An obscure instinct prompted her to say :

' I can't see her at the moment.   She was talking to another girl in the hall a little while ago.'

She saw the dark boy dip his smooth head suddenly and dart a kiss on Marigold's hair. Marigold looked vague, her eyes narrow, her lips half smiling.

' Shall we dance ? ' she said.

' Rather.   Love to.'   He got up with a show of alacrity.   ' Blue Danube, too.   We mustn't miss that.'

And they waltzed together to the music made for joy.   She danced with him in love and

sorrow. He held her close to him, and he
was far away from her, far from the music,
buried and indifferent. She danced with his
youth and his death.

§ 21

She hurried. She'd seen them when the
waltz was over, running upstairs, he pulling
Marigold after him lightly by the hand. Now
a fox-trot had begun. I must catch her before
she gets down again and gets lost.

She waited, leaning against the banisters. A
door on the top landing burst open. She heard
Marigold laugh softly in her throat and call
out ' No ! ' looking back over her shoulder as
she ran out.

' Marigold ! '

' Olivia, hullo ! . . . What d'you want ? '

Her voice was harsh. She looked startled,
staring rather blankly out of a flushed, somehow dazed face.

' Marigold, he's still waiting for you.'

' Who ? '

Her eyes with their dilated pupils opened
wide.

288

' The blind——'

' Oh——' A spasm crossed her face.
' Timmy ! Oh hell, I never went back. How
lousy of me. I did mean to too. I wanted to.
Have you been dancing with him ? Isn't he
sweet ? I think he's divine. Honestly, he's
about my favourite man. Isn't it a damned
shame ? . . . And I've never never heard him
complain. If it was me I'd shoot every one I
could lay hands on and then myself. But he
never seems to get the blues—he's always the
same. You simply forget about him being——'
Just as before, she wouldn't say the word. She
continued rapidly : ' His wife's awfully nice
too. She's really awfully nice—' she frowned—
' but you know—she's different,—I mean—if
one wanted to be snobby one would say so.
She was his nurse. She's about ten years older
at least. And so fearfully sensible and man-
aging. Of course it's a good thing, as they're
so poor, and him being like that—only it makes
you feel he hasn't any—you know—frothing
and frisking in his life. Perhaps he doesn't
mind. I suppose it was tremendous luck
finding some one willing to—— Not that you
could make a martyrship out of living with

such a darling. Still, I suppose it's not every one—I mean, a very young pretty person would probably make a mess of it. I mean loving wouldn't be enough. He wants somebody to take him for granted and make him feel ordinary and safe and practical, and she does that. They do seem to get on splendidly, and they've got a nice ordinary little girl. It's amazing to see him going about among the coops and things, on his farm, lifting the hens off and collecting the eggs, and picking up the tiny chicks when they scatter—he just seems to see with his fingers—have you noticed his hands?—and he never stumbles or makes a mistake. I go quite often. He loves being absurd and making silly jokes—only he needs starting off. Thank heaven you reminded me. . . .'

She had spoken as if out of a dream, as if scarcely aware of what she meant to do or say. But suddenly, at the sound of a door opening above her on the landing, she started, seemed to shake off a kind of haze.

' I'll go to him now this minute,' she said, with intense determination, staring downwards into the hall as if she could see him, as if she must see only him, and listen to no one else.

' I left him in the little room,' said Olivia.

The dark boy Rex came sauntering towards the stairhead, sleeking his hair. He didn't look pleased. She repeated :

' I'll go to him now.' And swiftly, without looking at him, she started to run away from him down the stairs ; seemed to fly and float in her airy skirts from landing to landing ; and vanished through the pillars.

Olivia went down slowly to the first half-landing. There was an armchair there which she had noticed earlier in the evening. It was covered in white velvet. It was empty and she sat down in it. I'm very tired. She heard the last reverberations of the dance roll far away from her. Not one blown flurry from one wave of it will reach me any more. I don't care any more. I don't mind in the least. To have come to the place of not caring was very soothing, very peaceful. . . . I've come to it because I'm not going away empty. I've had a lot really, one way and another. What was it that, at the last, had made almost a richness ? Curious fragments, odds and ends of looks, speeches. . . . Nothing for myself really. Rollo leaving me to go to Nicola. Rollo and his father smiling at one another. Peter crying, saying, 'Are you my friend? . . .' Kate looking so happy. . . . Waltzing with Timmy. Marigold flying downstairs to him. Yes, I can say I've enjoyed myself. Although my dress . . . She thought with longing of her dark bedroom, her bed waiting for her at home. I'm so tired. She went on thinking drowsily of white velvet, of its whiteness, its sheen and texture, thinking of the colour of her dress against it . . . red on white, blood on snow. . . . Yes. It's been *extraordinary*. . . . Her eyelids dropped. Half an hour passed.

§ 22

All at once the sober fox-trot flew off at a tangent, flung itself into a convulsion. *D'ye ken John Peel!* . . . mournful, gay, exciting. . . . What a noise of galloping feet! Shouting too. Faster and faster. With cries and stampings they came streaming in a tangle from the ballroom out into the hall. A few were trying to dance in their couples still. Tony and Kate.

Rollo with Nicola. But others had formed long galloping lines and were tearing about and cutting across everybody, huddling in bunches and unwinding again. Faster and faster. Maurice tearing up and down with the fluffy young person in pink ; so he'd managed that all right. . . . Etty and Podge, the Heriot twins and partners—Reggie, Reggie galloping for all he was worth, linked with a Martin upon one side and upon the other with Marigold. Reggie had compassed his objective. It was the fourth extra.

Sir John and Lady Spencer appeared together and stood by the ballroom door, smiling.

Then all at once the whole maze wavered, stopped dead.

God save the King.

§ 23

' Ha ! ' Reggie put down his empty cocoa cup. ' Comforting, comforting.'

Kate shook the thermos.

' There 's still a dreg. Have it ? '

She said it kindly. Conscience pricked her. I told him my programme was full.

'Well, if nobody else will. . . . Waste not want not, you know.'

Olivia thought of saying : Nothing wasted where you keep a pig. The Martins would have said it at once, most amusingly. Too late for me to start that sort of thing now. Besides, I can't be bothered.

Kate poured out the cocoa for him and replaced the flask on the hall table beside the biscuit box and the water jug and the envelope saying Lock front door and put out all lights. As if we needed to be reminded. But Mother would never trust one. Still it was funny really, nothing to be irritated about—rather endearing if one considered it in a detached way. She felt extraordinarily detached.

All the usual things, the furniture, the curtains, the way the light fell, Dad's old cap and Homburg hanging up together—all seemed unfamiliar and far away, but lovable too, and curiously impressive—turning strange aspects in a dream. I've left it all behind me. She looked at Olivia lying back on the settee, her eyes black and small with sleep. We won't be able to talk over the dance, exchanging every detail for hours and days. I can't share to-

night with her. Olivia's too young. She still
belonged among all these dwindled objects—
on that old trivial plane of experience. Poor
Olivia ! Too hypocritical to ask now, had she
enjoyed it ?—having forgotten about her all
the evening ; having maintained a tranced
silence in the taxi coming home.

Reggie yawned loudly.

' Bedfordshire, I think.' He got up and un-
buttoned his overcoat. ' Well, well, well—it
was a very enjoyable evening.'

' Yes, it was a good dance.' Kate yawned
too. ' I think every one enjoyed it.' She
added with warmth : ' I'm so glad you did.'

Probably I misjudged him. It was just shy-
ness that made him talk so much and not look
at us. I expect he's frightfully nice really.
Most people are. If I get married—ever—I'll
ask him to come and do the service. She
waited for Olivia to chime in with one of
her usual easy enthusiastic corroborations ;
just to round off the only little edge of
uneasiness.

' What's happened to the—wha' d'you call
it ? ' said Olivia drunkenly. ' No, not that,
the——'

' Olivia's asleep. Come on up, Olivia. You can't go to sleep here.'

' *Can't* I . . .' She got up suddenly. ' Look, it's nearly four o'clock.'

Kate put out the light in the hall.

' Don't make a noise.'

The stairs creaked under them. Olivia whispered, ' Oh, my stays ! ' and giggled feebly.

' This way,' they whispered to Reggie. ' Can you see ? There's a step here.' They whispered : ' Good-night. Ten o'clock breakfast. Good-night.'

The owls were hooting all over the garden.

§ 24

' Silver brocade,' said Olivia. ' Simply glittering. And masses of diamonds. She looked wonderful.'

Mrs. Curtis considered glittering silver brocade. Very striking, no doubt. Though there was nothing like black velvet ; particularly to show off jewels.

' And was Marigold looking attractive ? '

Kate described that frock ; but she seemed absent. For once it was Olivia who had, apparently, been the more observant. She kept on having to supplement.

'Any little ornament?'

'I can't remember,' said Kate. 'I don't think so.'

'A wreath of green leaves,' said Olivia. 'Rather like ivy leaves—very small.'

Mrs. Curtis considered a wreath of green leaves. Very unusual. Charming.

Kate looked at the clock. It was twelve o'clock. Emptiness had descended on the day. Reggie had left by the 11.30, rather silent, not looking very well, his eyes a bit bloodshot. They were sitting in the schoolroom. Mrs. Curtis had set aside the remainder of her busy morning to hear all about last night.

'And you danced every dance?' . . .

'Yes, I think so.'

Kate yawned.

'I didn't,' said Olivia. 'Not quite.'

'You stayed later than I thought you would.'

'Mm, fairly late.' Kate rubbed her hands over her eyes.

'Were you introduced to any one?'

'No, not a soul. . . . All the locals were there.'

' I was,' said Olivia. ' To several people.
One was blind.' She described Timmy.
' And one was an awfully clever boy called
Peter Jenkin. A poet. And one or two
others.'

Really, it seemed as if Olivia had had the
more interesting evening. Of course her
manner was easier than Kate's—more winning,
perhaps. One never could tell about social
success. She herself had always done better
for partners in spite of May's exquisite features.

' Did you speak to Lady Spencer at all—or
to Sir John ? '

' Only to shake hands at the beginning and
end.' Kate languidly added : ' She seemed to
think we looked all right.'

' Oh ? '

' At least she said how nice we looked, or
something.'

Well, that was satisfactory. Lady Spencer's
was an opinion one set store by.

' That's good.'

' I talked to her a bit,' said Olivia. She
decided not to mention the reel. Mother
wouldn't understand. ' And I talked to Sir
John too. He showed me some of his books.

298

He wanted to be remembered to Dad. He said he was a very able man.'

' Have you given Dad the message ? '

' No, not yet.'

' Well, don't forget to.'

' And I sat out a dance with Rollo. He's frightfully nice.'

Mrs. Curtis said very affably :

' I've always heard he is charming.'

Really, Olivia seemed to have done extremely well. A special score that Sir John should have noticed her, actually shown her his books. And Rollo too. . . . What was the matter with Kate? One might have made allowances on the ground of her feeling her late night, but that she looked so particularly fresh and blooming. A little jealousy could it be? . . . The younger sister——

The telephone bell rang. Kate jumped.

' Now, who can that be ? ' said her mother.

Kate had become very pink in the face. She made an effort.

' Wasn't it extraordinary finding Etty staying with the Heriots ? '

Violet appeared at the door.

' Miss Etty Somers to speak to Miss Kate.'

After a few minutes Kate returned, looking particularly composed and a little pale.

' Well, is she coming to see us to-day ? ' Mrs. Curtis spoke in her indulgent Etty voice.

Kate said with peculiar calm :

' The Heriots want me to dine and go to the hunt ball.'

Abruptly her mother's face altered. In a flash all was clear as day. She said quickly at random :

' When is it ? '

' To-morrow.'

' Just you ? '

' Yes.'

' We must talk it over.'

She got up to go, voice, manner her most authoritative, most non-committal.

' I said I could,' said Kate.

§ 25

Olivia went out into the garden. She hurried down the lawn, past the walnut tree, not stopping to swing, past the distant back view of Dad and Uncle Oswald taking their constitutional in the rose garden—two funny old brothers pacing together. And there was James, waveringly turning the shrubbery corner on his bicycle. She hurried on. When she got to the kitchen garden she started to run. Oh Kate ! She's not going to tell me. Everything's changing, everything's different. She ran for all she was worth down the path and out by the gate into the field. A pheasant burst out from the trees and shuddered into the air, clanking his raucous clockwork of alarm. She ran over the rough damp turf. I'm left behind, but I don't care. I've got plenty to think about too. Everything crowded into her head at once. Timmy, Marigold, Rollo, Nicola, Archie, Peter, Maurice—words, looks, movements—simply extraordinary. Life—— She felt choked. Oh Kate ! We won't tell each other. . . . She leapt across a mound. Everything's going to begin. A hare sitting up in the grass took fright, darting ahead of her into the ploughed land. The rooks flew up in a swirl from the furrows. All the landscape as far as the horizon seemed to begin to move. Wind was chasing cloud, and sun flew behind them. A winged gigantic runner with a torch was running from a great distance to meet her, swooping over the low hills, skimming from them veil after veil of shadow, touching them to instant ethereal shapes of light. On it came, over ploughed field and fallow. The rooks flashed sharply, the hare and his shadow swerved in sudden sunlight. In a moment it would be everywhere. Here it was. She ran into it.